Between
Sky & Sea

HERZ BERGNER was born in Poland in 1907. He migrated to Australia in 1938 and lived in Melbourne. Bergner was a prolific writer of short stories and novels, in Yiddish, about Jewish migrant life in Australia and the struggles of his people in Poland. His novel *Between Sky & Sea* was first published in 1946. Herz Bergner died in 1970.

JUDAH WATEN was born in Russia in 1911 and migrated to Australia in 1914. He lived in Perth as a child before moving to Melbourne in 1926, where he became involved with a group of immigrant Jewish writers. Waten wrote novels, short stories and memoirs. *Alien Son*, his most famous novel, was published in 1952. Judah Waten died in 1985.

ARNOLD ZABLE is a highly acclaimed novelist. His books on the experiences of immigrants in Australia include *Café Scheherazade*, *Jewels and Ashes*, *The Fig Tree* and *Scraps of Heaven*. His most recent novel is *Sea of Many Returns*. Zable was born in New Zealand in 1947. He lives in Melbourne.

Between Sky & Sea

HERZ BERGNER

Translated by Judah Waten
Introduced by Arnold Zable

TEXT PUBLISHING MELBOURNE AUSTRALIA

The paper in this book is manufactured only from wood grown in
sustainable regrowth forests.

The Text Publishing Company
Swann House
22 William Street
Melbourne Victoria 3000
Australia
textpublishing.com.au

First published 1946 in Australia by Dolphin Publications
This revised translation published 2010 by The Text Publishing
Company

Cover and page design by Susan Miller
Typeset by J&M Typesetters
Printed and bound in Australia by Griffin Press

National Library of Australia
Cataloguing-in-Publication data:

Bergner, Herz, 1907-1970.

Between sky and sea / Herz Bergner ; translator, Judah Waten.

ISBN: 9781921656316 (pbk.)

Waten, Judah, 1911-1985.

839.133

INTRODUCTION

Between Sky and Sea was first published in 1946. It went on to win the Australian Literature Society's gold medal for book of the year, but soon lapsed into obscurity. Its republication marks the resurrection of a lost classic of Australian literature, a novel ahead of its time, a work that speaks to the future while it honours the past.

Written in Melbourne during the final years of the Second World War, Between Sky and Sea depicts the voyage of a group of traumatised Jewish refugees fleeing Hitler's terror. The Greek freighter has been at sea for weeks, drifting helplessly in search of a port. The novel presents a microcosm of life in all its facets, from the crippling effects of trauma and the irritations of living in close quarters, to poignant acts of humanity and compassion.

Herz Bergner arrived in Australia in 1938. He was born in the Polish town of Radimno in 1907. His family settled in Vienna during World War I, and returned to Poland in 1919. During the inter-war years, Warsaw was the hub of Yiddish cultural life in Eastern Europe. Bergner's older brother, the writer Melekh Ravitch, was the long-serving secretary of the Yiddish Writers' Association. Almost every Yiddish writer of note spent time in its legendary premises. Bergner's stories first appeared in Yiddish periodicals in Warsaw in 1928. *Houses and Streets*, his first collection, was published in 1935. Herz Bergner served his writing apprenticeship when Yiddish literature was at its creative zenith.

But this was also a time of impoverishment and political turmoil. Hitler had come to power and the storm clouds of war were gathering. Bergner seized the opportunity to emigrate. He settled in Melbourne where there was a small but active community of Jews who maintained Yiddish as their mother tongue. In 1941 he published *The New House*, a collection of short stories set in Warsaw and Melbourne. The stories reflected Bergner's recent experiences and those of his immigrant readers. He writes of their journeys and the challenges of adapting to a new life.

The Holocaust was a demarcation point for Yiddish writers. *Between Sky and Sea* was one of the earliest fictional accounts of the brutal and inconceivable events of the times. The writing is propelled by a sense of urgency. Bergner wrote the novel in Melbourne as the news was filtering through that a catastrophe was taking place in the Jewish communities of Europe. His people were being enslaved and murdered, or forced into flight. And he was well aware of their plight. In January 1942, Bergner published an essay pleading the case for increased European migration to Australia. Once flourishing Jewish communities, he pointed out, were being wiped from the face of the earth.

Bergner would have known of the ill-fated voyage of the *St Louis*, the ocean liner that left Germany in May 1939 with over 900 Jewish asylum seekers on board fleeing from the Third Reich. The ship was turned back from Cuba and not permitted to land in the USA and Canada. The refusal prompted several passengers to attempt suicide and led to a near mutiny. As the *St Louis* sailed back to Europe, a group of passengers took over the bridge and occupied it until their rebellion was put down. Through intense negotiations and the support of the captain, Gustav

Schroeder, the passengers were able to disembark in Antwerp before the ship returned to Germany. Nevertheless, 254 of the passengers perished in the Holocaust.

The refugees on Bergner's fictional Greek freighter undertake their voyage several years later, while the war rages. They are trapped between sky and sea, and within the terrors of their recent past. They have lost entire families and witnessed the destruction of their communities. They have wandered through many lands and are tortured with guilt at having been spared the fate of those left behind.

With each day at sea they edge closer to despair. Their meagre rations of food decrease. Quarrels erupt. Malicious gossip takes hold in the idle hours. Those who succumb to disease are buried at sea. The passengers no longer know where they are. They are an unwanted people, and endure racist taunts from some of the crew.

When typhus breaks out on board, a seaman hisses: 'Human beings? Important people? You have been thrown out of everywhere and no one will take you in. All doors and gates are closed to you. We can't put in at any port because of you. Everybody is afraid you'll get your feet in and never go away.' The language is apocalyptic. There can be no compromise, no soft landings. The sea is a malevolent force, the sun an inferno, the boat a mobile internment camp. It is a voyage of the damned.

Yet the work is distinguished by its empathy, and by the resilience Bergner finds in his characters despite the perils they face. He does not idealise his ill-fated refugees, but depicts them as fallible individuals. He writes with irony, psychological insight and compassion. He presents a broad range of characters from the orthodox to non-believers, and exposes their flaws and obsessions, their hopes and uncertainties. He puts a human face to their suffering, revealing both their vulnerability and fierce will for survival.

And there are moments of redeeming humanity, acts of unexpected kindness. A Greek passenger returning to work in Australia, accompanied by a bride from his home village, converses with one of the refugees: 'You and me one fate,' he says, as he points to himself and nods to the Jewish passengers. He identifies with their trauma and sees himself as a brother in adversity.

Between Sky and Sea deserves its place as a significant Australian novel due to its literary merit and because it remains as relevant today as it was when it was first published. As I write there are millions of people on the move in search of refuge from oppression. Many languish in camps for years on end, while others are en route, prepared to risk all to gain landfall on firmer shores. Theirs are perilous journeys enacted anew in each age. Some make it and some don't.

On 19 October 2001, 353 men, women and children, asylum seekers fleeing Iraq and Afghanistan, drowned when their fragile fishing boat, now known as SIEVX, sank en route to Australia. There were just forty-five survivors. Bergner's fictional account of the fate of the passengers on board the Greek freighter is chillingly similar to survivors' descriptions of the SIEVX sinking. The two disasters, sixty years apart, one imagined, the other real, encapsulate the universal plight of asylum seekers. They highlight the fraught nature of the journey, and the desperate measures that people take to escape oppression.

The sinking of the SIEVX was the biggest post-war maritime disaster off Australian waters, yet it has been readily forgotten. This new edition of Bergner's novel is a timely reminder of the desperation that drives people to risk their lives in search of freedom. It highlights the luck involved in whether one survives the journey. But it is also a matter of government policy: at the time of the SIEVX sinking the Howard government was advising its navy personnel to force boats of asylum seekers back out to sea. Like Bergner's characters, they were consigned to live in limbo, their goal so tantalisingly close, yet agonisingly out of reach, the sea an insurmountable barrier.

The sea is a recurring image in Bergner's work. In an earlier story 'Ship-brothers', he dwells on the moment of farewell, when a group of Jewish immigrants casts off from Europe for their voyage to Australia. It is the point of no return. The story foreshadows some of the themes of the novel published five years later.

Translated by Judah Waten, the English edition of *Between Sky and Sea* preceded the 1947 publication of the Yiddish language original. Bergner was anxious to reach a wide audience. It was first published by Dolphin, a venture set up in 1945 by Judah Waten and the painter Victor O'Connor, with the aim of printing affordable editions of Australian books with progressive themes. Dolphin was one of the few outlets for Australian literary fiction at the time. One of its earliest publications, *Southern Stories*, featured Judah Waten's translation of Bergner's short story, 'The Boardinghouse'.

Waten spoke of the translation process and his friendship with Bergner: 'We worked together on translations. I didn't just translate away on my own.

Every Saturday we got together. And when you translate, you sort of looked into a word. It's like performing some kind of surgery.' Bergner was, says Waten, 'very odd because he wanted every word translated, and if the number of words came out fewer in English he wasn't very happy. He never really mastered the English language.'

Herz Bergner continued to publish Yiddish novels and collections of short stories until his death in Melbourne in 1970. Just one other novel, *Light and Shadow*, and several short stories were translated into English. *Between Sky and Sea* remains his masterwork.

Arnold Zable, 2010.

Between Sky & Sea

CHAPTER I

For five weeks the dirty, old Greek tramp steamer had drifted over stormy waters without sighting land. She creaked with age as she allowed herself to be tossed by the green waves that played with her like young children tormenting a senile old man. It seemed the ship had lost its way and would forever trudge across the seas. Nothing had been seen but sky and sea and the people on deck were weary of gazing into the distance, hoping that a fragment of land would swim into their vision. They were now accustomed to the steely glare of the sun during the day when they could not keep their eyes open, and to the blackness of night when they could not recognise each other. The order that no light was to be shown at night—not even a match was to be struck—had been given as soon as the ship sailed into the open sea.

On dark nights, when no moon shone, a solid tarry darkness surrounded the ship. She moved slowly like a black hearse and the Jews moved about aimlessly on the deck and the narrow worn steps of the spiral staircase. They groped with their hands as they stumbled against each other, unable to find a place to settle. Men looked for their wives and wives for their husbands. Children who had lost their mothers screamed in the black night and their cries spread fear.

'Mama! Ma-ma! Where are you, Mama?'

Good friends who talked for hours during the day passed each other like strangers. Suspiciously they allowed everybody to pass, recognising friends only by their voices. A familiar voice brought warmth and drew them together as if in new-found joy.

'That's Fabyash, isn't it?' One man stopped another, touching him with his hands and peering at him. 'Am I right?'

'Yes, yes, that's right. It's me, Fabyash. Why should a man be crawling around so late in the dark? It's too terrible to believe. You can feel the blackness with your hands.'

Although the captain had ordered them to stay in their cabins and go to bed early, they could not stay still; everyone was drawn outside. How could they go to sleep so early? From day to day things became worse. Food was supplied twice daily, but the dismal stew was shrinking and getting thinner.

Overnight new orders were born. Pasted on the rotting, greasy walls of the boat, notices screamed in strange big letters, crudely written. Then, one bright day, they found a new notice. It was cut from ordinary packing paper and still smelled of fresh ink. It ordered that water was to be used only for drinking. And another notice warned the crowd to remain quiet and not become alarmed.

Instead of calming the passengers, these last words cast a shadow of fear. People began to say that things must be bad: 'They won't admit how bad things are!' The passengers avoided the walls on which the notices were posted, afraid of new menaces. And in order to quieten their fears, they began to creep, uninvited, into each other's cabins. They talked about the countries they had wandered through since they were driven from their homes, and they outdid each other in knowledge of the new country for which they were bound—Australia. Although no one knew much, or had even heard much, about this new land, each one had a great deal to say about the country, its people and their customs.

Fabyash knew for certain that the country was surrounded by water on all sides and the people lived by catching fish, which they exported to the rest of the world. He was an energetic young man who always knew more than anyone else and nothing in the world could surprise him. He knew everything in advance, and he had a wealth of ideas about Australia. But Zainval Rockman could never stand Fabyash's boastings and with a wave of the hand he rejected this information. He was always looking for an excuse to show that Fabyash knew nothing and was nothing but a blatherskite. This time he really did talk Fabyash down and make him look small. He said that in the new country people made their living from timber. The country is still wild and has plenty of forests, so the people export timber to the rest of the world.

Hearing this, Mrs Hudess, a Warsaw woman who was proud that she came from a big city, rose from her place. She said neither Fabyash nor Rockman knew what they were talking about. The country rides neither on fish nor timber. Australia is a country like any other, with many big cities. Let Rockman and Fabyash stop talking nonsense and making Australia into a rural wasteland.

In order to support her words she called her two little daughters, who had gone to school and learned something about the matter. She loved to show her children off, whether it was the right time or not. She thought very highly of their talents.

But the daughters took no notice of their mother. As usual they were busy with their doll, which they carried about with them from morning till night. This doll was the only thing they had saved from the terrible event that had destroyed their home. Everyone had grabbed something, whatever he could, and they had barely escaped with their lives. Now the girls wouldn't part with the doll; they slept with her and took her walking, holding her hands as if she were a little child. The doll was old and worn and couldn't close its eyes when it fell asleep, nor could it utter its old cry when pressed in the stomach. The younger child spoke to the doll exactly the way her mother spoke to her whenever she saw her: overjoyed anew that her child had left behind all the horrors and now found herself in a safe place.

'My treasure…my precious.' The child caressed the doll just like her mother fondled her.

'Bless you. My heart swells when I look at you, and I saved you just by a hair's breadth. But where is your father? Where is my breadwinner? God in heaven save him!' And the little child clasped her hands, rolling her eyes to the sky, and pretended to wipe away her tears with her handkerchief, just like her mother did.

All day the children were busy, running around the deck, immersed in their own world. They had become so accustomed to the ship, the relentless sea and sky, that they could hardly remember the land. But the adults searched for the shore on the far horizons, in the sky and in the water, so that everything swam before their eyes. They suffered from seasickness, vomiting green gall until they hardly had strength to bear any more. Reb Lazar, the grocer, recited the psalms, intoned prayers from the sacred book, studied the Talmud and argued loudly that a Jew must never lose his beliefs, as long as life remained. A man must have faith, must trust in the Almighty! He told himself that he was not afraid of death if that was the Almighty's wish, if it was written in heaven so. But it is a pity for a Jew not to be buried in sanctified earth according to the custom.

And Fabyash shouted that it was his fate to die at sea instead of in his home which had been destroyed. He had been robbed of all his belongings, beaten down and left with only the shirt on his back. His heart bled every time he looked at his children.

'Me—well—never mind me! But what have the children done?'

He didn't believe the sea was safe and the Greek captain didn't look like a Greek to him. He could hardly bear to say it, but the captain looked like a German, an enemy of the Jews! It seemed to him that the gentile went about his ship silent and angry.

One day Fabyash ran down to the cabins, shouting: 'It's a story without an end! I swear the ship has turned back! With my own eyes I saw the ship turn round! I always said we'd have to watch the captain. Heaven knows where the gentile will take us yet. All he wants is to be rid of us Jews. I will bet anything that he is a German! He is as much a Greek as I am a Turk.'

The passengers had been wandering about the ship trying to give each other courage and unable to understand why the ship moved so slowly. Fabyash's words alarmed them for a moment, but they soon began to disagree with him, especially the women.

'Hold your tongue!' they shouted. 'The man has taken giggle-water and goes about babbling like an old woman. Look at the hero! A fine man you are! Fancy calling yourself a man!'

Fabyash couldn't escape from the women, nor could he say any more, so he kept his thoughts locked inside. He even refused to answer the distinguished Warsaw doctor who pestered him. The doctor was half senile and had long hair and a thick grey aristocratic moustache. He had been reminded of his Jewish ancestry by Nazi soldiers who had called him 'Hund kerl!' and 'Sau-jude!' and hanged his only son in his home before his eyes. Ever since, the doctor had refused to wash himself or to comb his long hair. He wandered around unkempt and dishevelled, his trousers unbuttoned and a half-mad smile on his face. His wife followed him with a wet towel, as a mother follows her child to wash its face and hands. On board the ship the doctor tried all the time to get closer to the other Jews. He stroked the children's heads and patiently listened to the women telling him about their illnesses. And always he made the same bitter joke to Fabyash.

'You don't feel like diving into the sea just now, Pan Fabyash, eh? The water must be wet.'

The doctor never left Fabyash alone; he was always peering into Fabyash's face with his foolish, good-natured smile and talking about his son as if he were still alive. But at the same time he had noticed, with passion in his tear-filled old eyes, a couple who never mixed with anyone else and were completely taken up with each other. The whole ship talked about them, amazed that a man and his wife who were no longer young were never seen apart, and that they looked as lovingly into each other's eyes as on the day of their wedding.

Nathan and Ida nursed the great sorrow that had overtaken them. Perhaps their pain was forgotten as long as they could sit close together for, deeply hidden, some joy lived within them. But they buried their happiness and cursed themselves for their sinful thoughts. They clung to each other, always with the excuse that they had to take care of each other.

From that time in Greece when the Jewish merchant had received them so hospitably and almost forcibly put them on the ship, they had been inseparable. They had stuck together while the ship floated, its rusty bowels creaking, tossed like a broken box on the frothing waters. Nathan was afraid to leave Ida for a single moment; she might do something terrible. In her agony she must always be able to turn to him, and he felt better sitting near her with only one wish in his mind: that the ship should never reach the shore where he would be forced to crawl back into life again. Better that the ship should remain eternally at sea.

On moonlit nights they would sit together looking at the water and watching the moonlight break over the waves like fragments of white glass, then pour like molten silver into the depths of the sea. Even when the sea was stormy and raged, opening great chasms, tossing the ship from side to side and covering it with foaming water, they would not retire to their cabins. They remained in a corner and watched how it became suddenly dark. A mist spread over the sea, joining it to the sky in a blanket of haze. Then lightning split the heavy bulging sky, like fiery whips, lighting the darkness and leaving the world for a moment in a blaze of light. The sea boomed with a thousand voices. Thunder reverberated across the sky as though iron-hoop barrels were being rolled, until it seemed that the whole world was quivering and breaking

Nathan and Ida liked to watch this wild game until their heads swam and everything danced and turned before their eyes. They stood behind the rope barrier that kept the passengers from the part of the deck that the waves flooded. Everyone else suffered from seasickness, but Ida and Nathan didn't suffer so badly and looked every danger in the eye.

Every time a wave washed over the deck as if to swallow the ship, Ida nestled closer to Nathan. He embraced her gently with the same emotion he had felt years ago when he had comforted her after her father struck her. Then he had stroked her dishevelled hair and felt her soft quivering shoulders. Her hot tears fell on his fingers, a tremor passed through him and he had been overcome with passion. Ida then realised that she was not indifferent to him. Although Nathan was her eldest sister's husband, she leaned closer and wished that his caresses would go on forever. So soothingly they healed the shame that her father had caused by striking her, a girl old enough to be a bride.

And now on the ship, where fate had brought them together, Ida felt happier by Nathan's side, although she would not admit it to herself and tried to stifle the truth. Just as Ida reminded Nathan of his home and his wife and child, so Nathan reminded Ida of her husband and child. They had very little to do with the other people on the boat; they always sat apart from them, absorbed in their own great sorrow.

Although Ida sometimes did not want to see Nathan, and sat alone in her cabin, he tried to keep her under his eye. And whenever the seas raged Nathan wanted her by his side on the deck, hoping that she would forget her troubles. In the presence of danger, he felt how close Ida was to him, and he thought of his wife and child who were lost when they fled from their home. And more than ever she reminded him of the years when she was a girl in her father's home, which was already falling apart even before it was destroyed by the Germans.

CHAPTER II

That had been many years ago in Warsaw when Nathan's father-in-law, Jacob, had a little leather shop attached to his home in Franciskana Street. Nathan was a student but he had abandoned his studies to look for a future because he had no strength left to starve. The name 'student' stuck. He was called the student in his father-in-law's house, and he was known by that name to the neighbours, and even to the children in the courtyard.

'Nathan, Jacob's son-in-law. The student with his pants torn.'

No matter how hard he tried to wipe away the traces of his student days, he could never get rid of that name. Jacob, a strong, plebeian man, made fun of him to his face but behind his back he boasted of Nathan's achievements, and God help the man who spoke a harsh word against him. Nathan knew that his father-in-law boasted of his 'refined, intellectual' son-in-law before the country merchants who came to his shop. He would pull out Nathan's student cap, long discarded, blow the dust off it, straighten out the gold braid and polish with his sleeve the shiny lacquered peak. He would hold the cap in his hand as though it were a rare antique and show it to everybody. But none of this was in Nathan's presence. To his face, his father-in-law mocked him, made fun of him, laughed at his delicate hands that still could not lift the heavy bundles of leather, although he, an old man, could lift them as if they were feathers.

Although Nathan worked beyond his strength, wanting to show that he was not just an extra mouth to feed, that he worked honestly for his wife and child, nevertheless Jacob called him the 'orphan child'. Nathan didn't fit in the house. He didn't get on well with his wife, Faigele, nor would he show himself anywhere with her. He had married her because he could starve no longer. He was quite unsuited to business; he did everything back-to-front and upside-down. Sometimes he attempted complicated business transactions, naively believing that he could trick the world. But the merchants caught him out immediately and he would look foolish and not know how to get out of the difficulty. Then sometimes he was honest—just an innocent soul. But neither one thing nor the other was any good for business, and in the end he could never judge a piece of leather.

It was the same in his relations with the people in the house. Sometimes he behaved humbly, spoke softly, and wouldn't touch a fly on the wall. But he soon saw that this wouldn't do, that he was being treated like a messenger boy, so he raised his head and told them not to forget who he was.

The only bright spot in the oppressive house— with its massive mahogany beds, huge wardrobes, the clumsy big table and the heavy grandfather clock that hammered out the hours sadly and monoto- nously—was Ida, his wife's younger sister. He thought she understood him and was sorry for him. At night he would sit reading a book and Ida would come in. When she stepped in from the street with the wind in her brown hair, her amber eyes half closed with girlish charm, her lower lip full and chapped, he felt all his aching yearnings disappear at once.

As soon as she came home, Jacob would shuffle out of his bedroom, fully dressed, for he would not close his eyes until his daughter returned, and burst out: 'Where have you been playing about, eh?'

He would push his cap up and down in anger. 'Where does a girl roam so late at night?'

Ida had graduated from college and wanted to study further, but her father would not allow it.

'I see no need for colleges. There is no future in that,' he shouted, and the neighbours would run out in amazement.

'No more college! I don't want another orphan child that can't tie a cat's tail. The Polish thieves won't allow a Jew to study. It's just a waste of time. You won't get anywhere with the Polish thieves.'

Ida became very stubborn and refused to eat. For weeks she would not enter her father's room. But Jacob kept an eye on her and knew her movements. When she wasn't about he searched her belongings.

Once, while he was standing reading a letter from one of her admirers, Ida came in. Her father pretended not to see her and continued to read the letter aloud, deliberately distorting the words so that they sounded comical. Then he saw her and pulled a frightened face, cheerfully pushing his cap back from his forehead, and innocently asked her: 'Who is this young man?' He pointed to a photo-graph. 'He looks like a madman from the asylum. Look at his clothes. Look at his face. He looks as if he hasn't had anything for breakfast.'

Ida grew pale with anger and her eyes narrowed to venomous slits. Furiously she spat out one word: 'Impudence!'

That was the end. Jacob was a hot-tempered and stubborn man, who was liable to use violence, even in the neighbourhood prayer house, if he didn't get his own way. He hurled himself at her and began to beat her. If Nathan hadn't dragged her out of his hands she wouldn't have escaped so lightly.

But her father won in the end. Neither her refusal to take food nor her disappearance from the house for weeks helped her. Jacob wouldn't give in and finally Ida married the man he wanted her to marry.

Ida changed after she left the house. She forgot Nathan's caresses which had so sweetly healed the wounds her father had inflicted on her. When she visited her parents' home she did not even glance in Nathan's direction. She had eyes only for her husband, gazing into his round, red face as if it were a mirror. She told her mother all about her baby, to the smallest detail, and sought her advice. And all the time she kept turning, with exaggerated affection, to her husband, who was always sleepy and smiling foolishly. She would straighten his tie and talk to him in a playful voice, turning up her broad, snub nose.

'Hershl, are you comfortable?'

'Don't eat so much, Hershl, or you'll get heart-burn. You glutton! You!'

Nathan understood her. He would not look in her direction, knowing that she was torturing herself to spite him. And when she could not hurt him, she would take it out on his child. She said the fair-headed boy was too thin, she didn't like the way he spoke, gabbling his words, nor did she like the clothes he wore. She didn't see that she was hurting the child.

Nathan was not offended, but his wife, Faigele, sat as if on hot coals, her normally calm white face flushed with sickly red blotches from shame and humiliation. And when Ida could find no more fault with the child or with anything else, she picked on her mother and complained about the crowded house where nothing was ever in its right place. She was always angry and complaining, and even when she played with the cat she blew into its ears savagely, tormenting the animal as she had as a child.

'Leave the cat alone!' Her mother couldn't stand it any longer; she couldn't understand what had happened to her daughter. 'Have pity! The girl hasn't improved a bit. As one is at seven, so is one at seventy.'

Sometimes Ida came uninvited to her father's business in the middle of the day. She dragged her little girl Sarah by her soft hand, angrily shouting at her. She would sit down at the table for hours as if she were a princess and watch Nathan lifting and carrying heavy bundles of leather.

Later Ida ceased coming to her parents' house altogether and Nathan didn't see her. Then he met her unexpectedly when his father-in-law's prayer-house politics proved correct and the German army besieged Warsaw.

Political discussion was as precious to Jacob as life. He often sat in the local prayer house far into the night talking with other Jews, and for his own opinions he would go through fire. He would even use his fists to prove that he was correct. He often became heated, saying that Poland was becoming too close to the Huns. He said they were kissing each other, dwelling together like doves. The Germans would entice Poland into a trap, and attack her when she least expected it. 'It is the habit of big fish to be friendly with little fish until they are ready to swallow them.'

Jacob had said, 'The Pole is going too far. He has become full brother to the Hun. He's learning from him to beat up the Jews. But his good brother will teach him a lesson yet. You can't play with the Hun. The German bandit will one day sit at the table in this house…'

Nobody paid much attention to him; most people thought he was rather foolish. But his timid wife gazed admiringly into his face. The lowliest uniform and the smallest brass buttons terrified her: once when a tram conductor came into the shop just to buy something, she was so overcome that she became faint and had to be revived. Having listened to her husband's grave pronouncements she began to store food away. You never knew what might happen… It wouldn't hurt to have it there…She didn't want to talk about it, for God forbid that the hour should ever come, but there would always be something for the children…She could well remember how it was in the last war…

When the German army stood before Warsaw, and the radio urged all young people to leave the city, Jacob commanded his children to flee. Every time Nathan came home from digging trenches, his father-in-law pleaded with him to go.

When, after several hours, the bombing ceased and people crawled like mice from the dark cellars, they were unable to look the morning in the face. And when they did, they could hardly recognise their streets, so changed were they.

Then Jacob started to pack. He threw off his long, black coat, rolled up his sleeves and tucked the fringes of his prayer shawl into his pants so that they wouldn't get in the way. In a great hurry he pulled an old suitcase out of the cupboard. He had inherited the suitcase from his father, and although the leather was old and cracked, it was still strong and could stretch like a concertina so that a world of things could be stored in it. He filled it to the brim, all the time remembering something else to take along. He didn't even forget Nathan's dusty prayer shawl bag, which he carefully squeezed in. Then, from somewhere he brought out a rucksack. When that was full he took a new linen sheet, tried it to see if it was strong enough, and made more bundles which he tied firmly with string. He emptied the kitchen cupboard of food, packing everything with great care. He allowed no one near him for he would rely on no one, and he even tricked his wife into going away to a neighbour's to spare her any heart-ache. He worked so hard that sweat poured from his face.

When everything was ready he picked up the heavy suitcase and ordered the children to leave immediately for it was dangerous to lose a moment.

When they insisted that he and his wife go with them, he refused to listen.

'I will end my days here,' he said, 'You go and God be with you. If everything passes over, and God wills it, there will be something for you to come back to...Go! Go, children. Don't delay.'

He kissed the mezuzah above the door and went ahead. Reluctantly the children followed him. It was a beautiful late-summer morning and the streets were lying shrunken and still, as if cowering in fear, waiting for another fiery deluge to descend from the sky.

Echoes of the deafening thunder which had shaken the world were still present and the streets trembled and breathed heavily as after an earthquake. Whole rows of houses lay in disorder, crumbled and sunk into the earth. Ruins crouched against each other and vast yawning holes stared vacantly and sadly from them. The walls were peeled and blistered like the faces of survivors of a terrible fire. Naked bricks bled from the peeled plaster and brick dust filled the air. Fiery tongues greedily licked the sky and tore pieces from it, covering the town in soot and smoke. Iron street lamps, as if in great pain, lay twisted like corkscrews. Tram tracks torn from the earth were bent and useless, and trams lay upside down like beetles with their bellies showing.

From ruins that were still collapsing the dead were being removed, covered with blood-stained clothes and sheets. The shrill cries of children and the shrieks of adults bemoaning the dead filled the air. A horse that had been unable to find shelter sprawled dead in the middle of the street, entangled in a shattered cart and partly buried under rubble. The front wall of a house had collapsed so that a room stood exposed to the street as if in a display window. Two beds were revealed, with big head-pieces, and pictures of an old father and mother hung on the patterned, rose-coloured wall. The childish faces of naked angels clutching lutes in their chubby hands looked down from the ceiling where they floated amongst the plaster clouds. The brass pendulum of a grandfather clock continued to tick off the hours as if nothing had happened.

That was how Warsaw looked when Nathan left it. Several times he tried to take the heavy bag from his father-in-law, but Jacob wouldn't give it up, saying that they had a long way to go and that there would be plenty of time for Nathan to carry it. So Nathan carried the rucksack on his shoulder and Faigele carried their child and Ida's, whose squabbling caused anguish to both mothers. Ida and Hershl carried the linen bundles between them.

Outside the city the family caught up with long columns of people, in wagons and on foot, who had fled Warsaw. They fell in with old-fashioned wagons, peasant carts and motor vehicles that were stalled by the dense crowds. Under their feet lay scattered bags and items of clothing that had been thrown away by people unable any longer to carry their loads. And all the time military trucks filled with soldiers tooted and cut their way through a mass of humanity that parted like open scissors. The trucks were hurrying to and from Warsaw, and when they had passed, the mass huddled together again in a tight knot. The column of refugees swelled as peasants with their cows and calves joined in. Then later it thinned again as many dropped out and were left behind.

The country road ahead gleamed in the sun. Somewhere in a barn a cock crowed, its noisy call fading to a sleepy cry. After the heavy thunder of guns and the long-drawn scream of screeching shells it seemed that the rooster's call came from a far-off, peaceful world that had ceased to be a long, long time ago. A soft haze shimmered in the summer air, caressing their faces like spider webs. The naked fields lay in vast coloured patches and trees had begun to shed leaves that burnt with the scarlet of sunsets. The golden autumn was coming; who knew whether Nathan would ever see it again?

They had gone a long way when Jacob stopped. He pushed back his hat, wiped the sweat from his brow and declared that it was time for him to go home.

'Mother won't know what to think!' he said.

He parted from his children calmly, asking only that his grandchildren grasp his long thick beard, which in his old age had begun to show a few grey threads. He was still the same as he had always been; he never for a moment lost his self possession. He handed the heavy bag to Nathan and said, 'Now! Be well, children. May the Almighty God be with you.'

And so he went away. His children watched him and saw his old broad shoulders swaying with strength and refusing to bend. He walked alone back to the city, pressing against the forward moving mass of people with their pitiful bundles. He never once looked back, but became smaller and smaller until he finally disappeared.

For three days and nights the column crawled on. The family walked—occasionally they hitched a ride on a wagon—until they arrived one evening at the tiny out-of-the-way village where the calamity occurred.

There was little evidence in the village that war

raged in the world. As if nothing had happened, the small dingy shops were still open, the peasants were selling potatoes and onions, and craftsmen were still at work. The refugees were received with bread and hot soup and little pots of coffee and milk to revive their flagging spirits. The Jews of the village were mostly artisans and market vendors with healthy sunburnt faces and necks. They said that, thanks to God, the war had not touched them. And even if the conflict came to them they would not flee.

Meanwhile the Jews took the new arrivals to the synagogue and made beds for them in their houses, saying that they must first rest their bones and tomorrow, if God willed, they would see what else could be done.

No sooner had these words been uttered than hell swept into the village and all that had been full of life was ablaze. And in the inferno Faigele and the children, together with Hershl, were lost.

Just before the German aeroplanes had come over the village like a plague of hungry locusts, leaving only desolation and death, Faigele left the synagogue to put the children to bed. Hershl went with her to help carry the bundles. They were going to the home of Reb Yidel, the fisherman and president of the synagogue. He was a big open-hearted

man with a long, thick beard and big swollen side-
curls, and around him clung the smell of the nets. He
had a booming voice to match his big body and he
threw open his home to everybody.

'Come to my place and have something to eat,'
he shouted from the door of the synagogue. 'My wife
has prepared the beds. It's your home, friends! Come
in and put your children to sleep.' He himself helped
the women carry their children to his house.

When the aeroplanes disappeared it became
silent, and Nathan rose as if from a terrible night-
mare. He was still holding the heavy bag tightly
against his body as if it were the dearest thing in the
world. It seemed to him that he was clutching his
wife and child to protect them against all evils.

He pushed the bag from him and ran to find
his family. But he found only Ida, his sister-in-law,
who was searching for her child and husband. She
wandered amongst the burning ruins, where fire
leapt from one wooden cottage to another, devour-
ing everything so quickly that it seemed it had come
to the village just for a little while and was in a hurry
to do the same terrible work somewhere else. All the
houses were soon in the midst of the inferno, and they
stood patiently like sacrificial heifers paying penance
for some terrible sin. The naked rafters and uprights

of the burning houses stood exposed like bones and ribs. Each house lit the night until it collapsed as if made of cardboard.

Ida still searched for her child and her husband, and now she was just like her mother. There was the same frightened face, the same movements and the same hoarse, high-pitched voice with the sob in it. The old Ida with the light brown hair and the amber eyes, which sometimes screwed up in malice, had disappeared, and she was half her size, shrunken into the little body of her mother.

'Where is my Sarah?' She screamed and called to her child as she tore her hair and pinched her cheeks. 'Where has my only child gone? Hershl! H-er-shl! Why have you left me alone?'

But nobody answered. There was only the crackling of fire, the sound of cannonfire, which came ever closer, and cries and shrieks that rose to heaven. People searched for each other amid the devastation, distraught and screaming, and they urged each other to leave the town because the German hordes were coming nearer.

Ida's cries cast a pall of horror over Nathan, deadening his own pain. He didn't know what to do. He dared not approach to reassure her that her husband and child might still be found hiding somewhere about. So Ida stumbled alone amongst a double row of burnt and naked chimneys, silvered by the shining moon, which lined the only street of the village. In place of the small cottages, they stood like rows of tombstones.

If not for Reb Yidel, who was scrambling amongst the ruins with the rescued Sefah Torah in his hands, Ida would never have left without Sarah and Hershl. He ordered the people to leave the town and hide in the woods. The fisherman suddenly appeared before Ida, stormed and shouted at her and commanded her to leave immediately with him. She was overawed by his imposing appearance and his thick untidy beard, which now looked broader and more disorderly and shook fiercely. She was frightened of his anger; his changed voice rang out with such authority that she went with him.

Without any will of her own she joined the people, who carried her along into the night, who jostled and pushed her far, far away from her husband and her child—over foreign countries and seas. There was no way back ever.

But Nathan was always by her side, never letting her out of his sight. Of Faigele and Hershl and of the children no news ever came, although Nathan and Ida always asked after them. They searched for them

amongst the people on the road; they asked everyone, describing them fully. But no one knew of them,
nobody had seen them.

CHAPTER III

The ship ploughed on and still no land was seen. Every night Ida and Nathan saw the moon pour its silvery coins wide over the surface of the water before they disappeared into the fathomless depths of the sea. When a storm came they didn't go to their cabins as the others did, but watched the sea changing and swelling. It took on an iron-grey visage and shrank and towered to leap upon the ship, driving her to one side as if to turn her over. And as often as the sea changed, so did Ida. Sometimes she was in a good mood, her face untroubled, and around her full, wind-cracked lips played the mischievous smile that Nathan had not seen for so long. She was full of charm and wrinkled her wide, snub nose and screwed up her eyes until only two smiling, amber slits could be seen. Her face was smooth and browned by the sun and wind so that it glowed like golden honey. Then she would behave exactly as she had when she was a school girl. She talked to Nathan with a child-ish drawl and gave herself airs, forgetting everybody and everything.

But this wouldn't last long. It was enough for Ida to see Mrs Hudess's two little girls carrying their doll around the ship for her to burst out crying. She found in them many similarities to her little Sarah. Then she drove Nathan away and made him the scapegoat for the bitterness in her heart, as if he was responsible for everything. She didn't want to see him again, torturing him and herself because they had run away from the village. They should have remained there and not been afraid of the Germans! Why had she become so frightened of that fisher-man? Who gave him the right to shout and order her about! And why had she obeyed him like a small child? Why was she so afraid for her own skin?

Ida became frantic; her tall, full figure quivered and she threw all the blame on Nathan, demand-ing he tell her why he had run away. He was a man; why was he so frightened? A fine man indeed, who was so afraid for his own life! Perhaps he was sick of his own wife and child.

Having spoken these words, she seemed afraid of them and stopped, completely bewildered. But soon she became accustomed to them and she began to hurl them with more malice until she was satiated and only then did she become silent. The worst she could say she said, and she enjoyed insulting him ever more grievously. Nathan then saw the Ida of old, after her father had forced her to do what he had wanted. In order to stifle her own misery and above all to conceal her love for Nathan, she had stopped at nothing. Everything seemed right to her and she constantly tortured herself and him.

Everywhere they went, through foreign countries and cities, Nathan had put up with the same thing, and it was hell for him. On top of his suffering and his constant yearning for his wife and son he had to listen to Ida's accusations. In torturing herself she seemed to find pleasure and relief and it was difficult for him to quieten her. She would cry for hours, lacerating her wounds, and he was helpless. He caressed and embraced her, and he felt her hot tears on his flesh. Then she became so yielding in his hands, so intimately soft, that a warm glow spread through every fibre of his body and in a second he could forget himself so completely that he could have embraced her passionately. Still she would not be calm and again she hurled those venomous and hurtful words which poured so easily from her tongue.

That the ship plodded on and on without an end seemed of no concern to them. They felt no hunger and they didn't notice that the portions of stew were getting scantier and they were no longer provided with even mouldy fish. Nathan didn't notice that his tall, spare body was getting thinner and his soft, grey eyes and his nose were getting bigger, his nose sticking out hungrily from his hollow, unshaven cheeks. Neither of them noticed how Fabyash ran frantically around the deck shouting that he knew for certain that the ship was turning back. 'The sun is rising in a different position now and that is proof that the ship has changed its course,' he demonstrated to the other passengers. The captain, that enemy of Israel, must be a German. We've seen things like this before. We should get together and give him a bribe. He's just the man to take a bribe.

But they wouldn't listen. They didn't want to believe him and they waved him away.

'God knows what he is talking about, the mad babbler!' said Zainval Rockman, shrugging his shoulders. Rockman had never had any opinion of Fabyash's knowledge and theories for he was a man who kept his pride and remembered his position. He wouldn't stop to talk to just anybody.

'A man gets an obsession and then he walks around like a bogeyman frightening children. I wouldn't give a farthing for his talk. Bah! What does he know?'

But the passengers would creep out on to the deck to convince themselves, with their own eyes, that Fabyash was right and the sun really rose from a different direction, although they still shouted him down and would not let him open his mouth. Mrs Hudess, who was afraid of nobody and spoke her mind to everyone, went for him and would give him no peace. She called her two little daughters to her, stroked their heads and held them in her thin, shrunken arms which yet retained their motherly comfort and warmth. And in her gentle drawl that could move a stone, she said to Fabyash, 'What have you against these two poor orphans, I ask you?'

Pointing to her little daughters, she went on, 'Why do you wish them harm? They still have a big world before them. Ghoul that you are, you haven't a human heart within you!'

Fabyash shot a despairing glance at the girls. He couldn't make out what Mrs Hudess wanted of him and he quickly got away from her. But still the people gave him no rest and he couldn't get away from them anywhere. From day to day he seemed to get smaller and smaller. His movements became more convulsive and his dark eyes darted anxiously to and fro like frightened mice in a cage. He rushed from one end of the ship to the other and could find no rest. He was so afraid that he hid from the lifeboat drill. Nor could he imagine how Reb Lazar could have such fortitude, such a delicate and refined man too! He walked about as if nothing was happening, studied the sacred books, recited psalms and admonished the others to have faith and place their trust in God. His only sorrow was that he might not be buried in sanctified soil.

Fabyash avoided him and wouldn't even look in his direction. He also avoided the distinguished Warsaw doctor who followed him everywhere and gave him no peace. The foolish, gentle smile on the doctor's unshaven, neglected face was always before his eyes and it seemed to Fabyash like the peaceful, innocent smile on the face of a corpse that has long left the land of the living.

But the doctor didn't see that Fabyash was avoiding him. Lately he had become cheerful and he wanted to talk to Fabyash. He talked constantly of his son whom the Germans had hanged before his eyes and of eminent doctors who had been his comrades, just as if they were all alive and on board the boat with him. He wandered about amongst the women and listened to them talking of their illnesses. He spoke in an elegant and measured Polish with many Latin words and phrases, as if he were reciting from memory, and the women didn't understand one word. He also used a few Yiddish words, which he pronounced like a proselyte, to show that after all he was a staunch Jew. He liked to explain to the women the causes of their illnesses and to analyse everything carefully. He became so absorbed in his talk that he didn't notice that everyone was edging away from him. When some of the women put a few coins into his hands he pushed the money away with an aristocratic air of disdain.

'Money—dirt,' he said in Yiddish, laughing himself at his pronunciation of the words.

Every day he neglected himself more. He didn't wash and he didn't comb his long, silvery hair. When his little, thin wife pursued him with a wet towel, like a mother chasing an overgrown child, he pleaded with her: 'Let me be, my dear. Can't you see that I am busy? I have just washed. Believe me, dear, believe me I have.'

Then he pulled down over his eyes his black,

broad-brimmed artist's hat which, as if in spite, was brand new. He loved to wear it. With quick, impatient steps he hurried away as though in haste to attend a patient.

In the big, dirty dining room there were a few wooden tables scattered with faded domino sets and chess boards. Here Nathan frequently met the doctor. Although there was now very little on the plates that were served here, the room was always noisy and full of people. Everyone turned anxiously to look towards the fat, olive-faced cook, with the dirty, white cap on his head every time he showed himself at the window. It was hard to find anywhere to sit. Ida and Nathan sat together with an old, partly deaf Greek and his big, timid wife and read all the names and dates scratched on the table. When Nathan found a Jewish name amongst them it seemed warmly intimate to him as though he had met an old acquaintance who spoke to him in his own language.

The Greek interpreted for Nathan the many notices and announcements on the ship. But Nathan understood him only with great difficulty, through his face and his gestures, for the Greek used a mixture of languages and was greatly perturbed when the Jews could not understand him. To add to his difficulties he was driven to talk to people, to unburden his heart.

After much effort Nathan learned that the Greek was going back to Australia where he had lived for many years. He had a cafe in a small town and he had been getting on quite well. But he couldn't find a wife there, for the girls made fun of him whenever he approached them. And he was not attracted to the Australian girls anyway; he couldn't look at the waitresses who made eyes at every diner. So he had been anxious to bring out a girl from his own home town and had saved shilling by shilling for the day when he could travel home and bring back a respect-able girl, a real Greek beauty. But meanwhile he had grown old and unluckily he made his journey just before the war. Now he was taking back with him a wife from his birth place. But who could have a mind for a wife when his country had been overrun? Although he was no longer young he wished he could return and be of some use to his people.

While he was talking, his wife looked him straight in the face with her large, tragic eyes. She also was no longer young. She was big and dark and in her slow movements she reminded one of a big, black horse. Her husband stroked her head with his toil-worn hand, hard from perpetual dishwashing. Then he straightened his own thin downy hair and gazed helplessly from his dark, squinting eyes over the dining room, ashamed of his deafness before his wife.

'Don't shout too much,' he always interrupted Nathan, 'I can hear, you don't have to shout. What do you think I am, deaf? I don't want that added to my troubles!'

All the same he watched Nathan's eyes so intently, to read what he said, that he was always covered in sweat. It pleased him to show the Jews that he was a brother with them in their adversity, that he suffered as they did. Every few words he spoke he repeated in English, feeling certain that the Jews must understand that language.

'Me and you, one fate.' And he pointed to himself and nodded to the Jews.

Although it was hard work for Nathan, he liked to sit and talk with him. When the Greek sat over the radio and listened helplessly with his deaf ears to the news of his overrun country a paternal care enveloped him. He looked after the decrepit old radio as if it were an antique treasure that he could not bear to leave. The radio croaked hoarsely, gave forth sounds as if it were in great pain and then was suddenly struck dumb and breathless, but he would not leave it. He listened closely to it, looked at it as if it were alive, talked to it, became angry with it and shouted and clenched his fists.

Ida had no patience with the Greek and was always urging Nathan to leave him or she would go away on her own.

And she did go away. She ran, taking longer and quicker steps until Nathan could hardly catch up with her. The merest incident, the slightest word, and she was offended. She was always ordering Nathan about in her husky, mannish voice and if he ignored her she became very excited. It was impossible to reason with her, for no sooner was she crossed than she was ablaze.

For whole days she would lie on her top bunk in the cabin, unwashed and uncombed, and she would allow no one near her. Curled up in a ball she lay half awake and drenched the bedclothes with her tears. She would not touch the food that Nathan with great difficulty obtained from the cook.

Once when Nathan climbed up to her bunk he jammed his finger and winced with pain. But she didn't stir; she didn't even look at him. Then she laughed through her tears, laughed with malice. She was glad that he was hurt.

'Why don't you wash yourself? Why don't you comb your hair? Look at your face! Why do you behave so badly?' Nathan implored her.

But she didn't answer him. It was as though he talked to the wall. Then, from her full, chapped lips came peals of laughter while her blazing, amber eyes flashed with pleasure, as if his unhappiness lightened her misery.

Suddenly she sat up and began to spit out pieces of truth which cut like sharp knives. She complained that Nathan never left her alone. Why did he follow her like a shadow? Why didn't he remember his wife and child whom he had left in the fire without any protection? Why had he attached himself to her? Why not leave her alone? Hershl and her little Sarah never left her mind for one moment.

Quickly she uttered these words as if to get rid of them, grinding them out as though the words hurt her and scalded her tongue and by getting rid of them quickly her heart would be eased.

When he heard her words Nathan stopped, bewildered and at a loss. He felt helpless and it seemed to him as though someone had undressed him and left him naked amongst strangers. He had tormented himself enough. All the sorrows and persecutions of the people who had stayed at home were deeply etched on his uneasy conscience. In Greece, at the home of the Jewish merchant who had treated them so handsomely, given them a roof over their heads and supplied them with everything for a long while, Nathan had not been able to rest. He had always in his mind the persecutions of his people and held himself to blame, although he knew it was foolish to think like that. Why had he run away like a coward? What had he done to deserve a good time when others were suffering so? Why was he so chosen! If only he hadn't run away he could be nearer to his own people. This was why he hadn't wanted to get on the ship for Australia when the merchant had fixed everything up for them. How could he deserve better than his child? How could be deserve better than his wife, Faigele, who had paid for everything?

As he thought of Faigele his heart shrank. What did she ever get from him? All the time they were together he had remained a stranger to her. He had never shared his plans with her, never talked intimately with her. She accepted everything as if it were her fate. She suffered in silence as though she had not earned the right to anything better. A proud woman, she had said nothing to him, never worried him with a complaint.

His thin, fair-haired little boy had seemed to understand him. This child, who had inherited the calm and patience of Faigele, had felt that his father was not on the best terms with his mother, that there was something wrong between them. The boy felt that his mother was unhappy and would not leave her side, as though he wanted to take his father's place. He had always looked pleadingly at Nathan, from his soft, grey eyes, as if begging his father not to be unkind to his mother. Once, while Nathan was gazing at Ida the boy had come to him and awakened him as from a dream, diverting his father's gaze from his Aunt Ida, and had taken him into the room where his mother was.

Now Nathan saw his son before him, felt his warm, bony hand within his own and heard the child's soft voice calling:

'Come to Mother, Father; Mother wants you. She sent me to call you.'

Nathan left Ida's cabin, determined never to see her again. They must never meet again, he thought; they must never see each other again.

CHAPTER IV

For a few days they did not see each other. Nathan did not appear on deck, but sat locked in his cabin and Ida lay in her bunk. When Nathan could no longer stand his cabin, where the air was thick and heavy to suffocation point, he found a spot on the deck and sat there all day. The sickly, salty odour of the sweat and dirt of the many people on board who had not washed themselves for weeks and had slept packed into dark cabins clung to every wrinkle of his face and hands and every fold of the clothes the Jewish merchant in Greece had given him. Even out in the air the sour odour would not leave his clothes, now threadbare and grimy, that hung loosely on his bony body and made him look like a boy in his father's clothes.

Nathan sat in a corner in the dark until late at night and when he returned to his cabin to go to sleep he noticed that someone had been at his bunk. His bed had been aired and made and the straw pillows had been shaken up and tidied. It was easy to see that a woman's hand had been there.

Nathan lay awake all night. Unrest had seized him and prevented him from closing his eyes although he was tired. He lay as if suspended in mid-air, not wanting to lose the faint but familiar feminine scent, reluctant to disturb the bedclothes that a feminine hand had so devotedly arranged.

It was only towards morning that Nathan fell asleep. He slept heavily without stirring until well into the day and when he awoke he felt as if he had overslept a very important engagement. Then he saw a freshly washed shirt near his bunk. Last night in the darkness he had not noticed it.

Nathan took in his hand the shirt which was stiff from salt water and he remembered everything from the previous night. The joy that had been interrupted by a few hours' sleep enveloped him. The shirt that Ida had washed for him still held the touch of her fingers despite the odour of sea and salt. He stroked the shirt which she had held, was loath to wear it and hung it again where he had found it.

Still he did not go to her cabin. Several days passed during which he knew all her movements and even what she thought of doing. But he avoided her, did everything in his power not to meet her. And when he stood before the door of her cabin, he could not bring himself to open it.

Often while he stood there, unable to make up his mind whether to go in or not, he encountered Bronya, a plump, pretty young married woman who slept in the same cabin as Ida and who preferred to speak only Polish. These accidental encounters appeared to startle Bronya, who drew back with a surprised shriek.

'Goodness, how you frightened me!'

'Excuse me. Sorry.'

But Nathan noticed that the whole thing was not so innocent, that Bronya was watching him from behind the door. She had discovered that he and Ida were not a married couple and she kept an eye on them with feminine curiosity, never letting them out of her sight. Now everything became clear to Nathan. He had taken no notice of Bronya at all and this had annoyed her because she was accustomed to men noticing her and paying attention to her.

Bronya was the wife of big, broad-shouldered

Marcus Feldbaum, who had been dubbed 'the ox' on board the ship because of his large, watery dull eyes and his enormous hands and feet, and because he was frightened to death of his wife and had no idea of the tricks she played behind his back.

Although Feldbaum had been a well-respected citizen at home, where he had owned a good many acres of land near Lvov in Galicia, he behaved simply and was friendly with everybody. He was slow and stolid, with much of the Ukrainian peasant in him and nothing in the world ever angered or excited him. He never interfered in anybody else's business and so he was hardly noticed on the ship. He wore a green shooting cap, riding breeches and high boots and smoked coarse tobacco which he rolled himself just like the Ukrainian peasants. He guarded his tobacco like the eyes in his head. But he had one weakness and that was food; he liked to eat a lot. And in these hungry days on the ship when the only meal of the day was a little soup with beans or barley, he suffered a great deal. He felt hungrier than most people and his big body constantly clamoured for food and became thinner from day to day. Feldbaum became emaciated and the skin on his face hung loosely in little bags and from his big, cloudy eyes shone the pain of a starving ox. He was a completely changed man. He dreamt only of food and remembered all the time how his wife had cooked delicacies for him. He could still taste the brown Galician pies stuffed with black maize and meat, the crisply fried pieces of chicken fat, the red Ukrainian borsht cooked with a fat marrow bone and the Hungarian meat jelly with garlic and pepper which he loved as much as life itself.

Bronya was the very opposite of her husband. She came from a poor tradesman's family and no sooner had she married well than she began to behave completely above herself and went to town in a britzchka every day. She never put a foot over the doorstep of her parents' poor home, but she ran to every Polish theatre and dance hall. She was gaudily dressed in frocks and hats from the most expensive shops. Only one thing poisoned her life—she was afraid of her brother, Noah, the carpenter's assistant. She was very much ashamed of him and to make it worse he was a 'Red'. Once, when he met her in the street, he upbraided her for not assisting her parents and making him shoulder the whole burden of the household.

Even on board the ship her brother, who had come with them, worried her. Nothing that she did pleased him and he was always on her husband's side.

But Bronya didn't take much notice of him. She played the same part as she had at home, promenading the deck with all the assurance of a handsome woman who knows that men will make sacrifices for her. Although everyone else's clothes were ragged and torn and no one had much heart for dressing up, Bronya still found something with which to adorn herself. She dug up coloured ribbons and bits and pieces to decorate her person and to bind her thick, black hair. As she walked she swung her full hips and revealed her rounded throat, so fully displayed that her breasts, pressed together like two ripe apples, furtively peeped out. The sailors, hungry for women after long weeks at sea, devoured her with their eyes, measuring the worth of every part. They winked suggestively at her, called her a temptress and talked obscenely amongst themselves to appease their hunger.

'She's worth a sin.' They smacked their lips as over a tasty morsel. 'Devil take the Jews, but there are some pretty women amongst them. It would be worth a month's pay to sleep with her for just one night!'

But Bronya didn't look at them, although, to tell the truth, it gave her pleasure when their eyes followed her. To spite them she swung her full hips

more provocatively and passed so close to them that
their heads almost began to swim—but that was all.

One might almost have thought that she had
no interest in men. But the whole ship knew that
Bronya wasn't quite as innocent as that; that every
night when it became dark she dressed herself in her
coloured bits and pieces, combed her hair carefully
before the broken and blackened mirror from which
she never parted and met the tall, elegant steward.
In a corner hidden from prying eyes she sat with him
until late into the night. And it was not all for love!
For from him she got biscuits and chocolates which
she was always pulling out of her pockets to eat. As
a result her cheeks were still round and rosy while
those of all the other women were emaciated and
sunken. Although all the rest of us are starving, they
said, no one else sells herself.

She would never have been forgiven if she had
kept for herself all the good things she obtained
from the steward, but she was often pushing the
delicacies into the hands of the small children on
the ship. Bronya herself had no children and she
longed for them. She loved to play with the children
and invented all sorts of games for them. But
especially she liked the little girls. She dressed
them up as she dressed herself, in the same coloured

ribbons and pieces, loved to comb their hair and encouraged them to look into her worn mirror to admire themselves. To these children she gave some of her chocolates and biscuits.

For this Bronya was forgiven everything. Averting their glances, the passengers discussed among themselves whether it would be right to send her to the captain to make enquiries for them. It was none other than Fabyash who suggested this and he argued with great passion:

'Perhaps...Perhaps she will find favour in the captain's eyes.'

Fabyash's small, black eyes blazed with conviction and they glanced quickly here and there as if they wanted to run away.

'Such a lively person! Such a beauty! When the captain sees her he will become as gentle as a lamb. And at last we will know whether we will be allowed to land somewhere or whether we must die on the sea! This is a story without an end. It is unbearable!'

Nathan had heard but not heeded some of these stories of Bronya. They had never been of any interest to him and they had never stayed in his mind. But now before Ida's door where he stood with Bronya, he remembered them all. So as not to direct attention to himself and Ida, he decided to go into her cabin quickly. Bronya looked at him knowingly, with the glance of a sinful wife who loves to catch everyone else at the critical moment so as to appear innocent and free of her own sins.

Nathan went in to Ida and found her lying on her bed exactly as he had seen her when he left her several days ago. It was as though she had not left the bed in all that time, not moved from that position. When he entered she hardly raised her eyes as if it was no surprise to her that he should come back. She had been certain of it from the beginning.

Without a word, Nathan sat down by her side, and she spoke to him in an ordinary tone, as though she was resuming an interrupted conversation. Her alarm at his sudden disappearance, that had not left her for a moment, vanished as he sat down and she was no longer interested in him or anything else.

But she wasn't too tired to continue to talk about Hershl, Sarah and her father and mother somewhere in Poland.

'Who knows what has happened to them? Are they still alive?' Not one reply had come to all the letters and postcards they had sent from Greece. Little Sarah constantly came to her in her dreams. With arms outstretched from the fire, she called to her, 'Mama...Mama, save me. Why have you left me? I suffer such torment, Mama!' And even now that she was awake she could still hear her child's pleading voice. She saw still the hands outstretched from the fire and she cried aloud with pain, covering her eyes. She covered her ears with her hands, feeling that her misery was beyond her strength to bear.

Ida slowly sat up on her bed and idly smoothed the pillow, while she drew out a piece of narrow, pink ribbon. Nathan felt a stab of pain in his heart as he recognised the hair ribbon that little Sarah had worn when they fled from Warsaw. Ida had never shown it to him before and now that he saw it he became afraid. She caressed the ribbon in her hands, made a bow and soon untied it. She told him how she had tied it in Sarah's dark hair and looked to see if it matched the child's blue eyes. Then something had told her heart that it was the last time she would plait her child's hair. Her heart was heavy and throbbed with longing. Ida repeated her mother's saying: 'The heart never lies. It always knows everything beforehand.'

She could not remember how it was that she had the ribbon now. Her memory had become weak. All she knew was that she would never again plait her child's hair.

Nathan didn't answer her or disturb her with a movement, but he looked intently at her. The sight of Sarah's ribbon in this cabin had deprived him of speech and he sat as if stunned. He didn't know what to do. Then a light knock on the door was heard and Bronya came in quickly, without waiting for an answer. She pretended to be startled and hastily drew back, asking in an exaggeratedly genteel voice,

'Am I permitted...may I enter? Oh, pardon me, have I disturbed you? Believe me, I didn't know, God protect me. I am not one of those people who stick their noses into other people's business. God forbid!'

She pursed her lips and spoke a strange Yiddish dotted with German and Polish words. She pretended that she wanted to leave but remained rooted to the spot and her eyes swept over everything looking to discover what was taking place. All this time she stood by the open door, which she had deliberately left ajar so that anyone could freely look in.

Nathan's blood boiled and his face grew red. It was only with difficulty that he restrained himself from throwing her out. He couldn't understand how anyone in such tragic times could behave so badly or be concerned with such trivial things.

On the following day the whole ship knew that Ida and Nathan were not married and after that their every step was watched. Everybody looked at them with knowing smiles and during the long, empty days they had something to concern themselves with and something to talk about.

CHAPTER V

No sooner had Nathan and Ida ceased to be the main topic of conversation than a new event stirred everyone deeply.

Mrs Hudess and her two daughters and Fabyash and his wife and children were involved.

An altercation broke out on the ship and two factions came into being. One group was on the side of Mrs Hudess and the other supported Fabyash.

Fabyash flew around muttering and heaping curses on himself.

'What good did it do me?' he shouted. 'How could it help me?'

But turn back he couldn't. He felt small in his own eyes and he told himself that he had fallen in the estimation of all the other men.

'When one falls,' he said to himself, 'one falls to the bottom.'

Fabyash felt guilty and he told each one separately the same story. He said he could no longer watch the suffering of his little boy. The poor child was fainting from hunger and he had had no choice. He had fallen so low as to take a biscuit from Mrs Hudess's little girl and give it to his son. He felt that the little mite was dying; what was he to do? So Fabyash defended himself.

'What is all the row about? What have I done? In what way did I sin? As a matter of fact I did not trick the biscuit away from the child as Mrs Hudess says. It's a lie! As a matter of fact the child left the biscuit on a step.'

Although nobody really believed his story and secretly thought that Fabyash had tricked the biscuit out of the child's hand, nevertheless even Fabyash's enemies looked aside and let him get away with his story. Only Mrs Hudess would not remain silent. She was excited and interrupted his talk.

'Found it. Found it,' she mimicked him in a honeyed, innocent voice. 'Look at the simpleton! Look at the holy man in his white collar! One would almost think he is innocent as a dove. Pearls pour from his mouth. It's as well that the child's a witness.'

Mrs Hudess was not slow to call the child to be a witness and meanwhile she held Fabyash.

'Liar!' she shouted at him. 'May you live to speak one word of truth, you are a thief through and through. Coming as he does from amongst the Gerer thieves how can one believe a word he says?'

But this was going a bit too far and although Fabyash didn't have many close friends and everybody got a little pleasure from hearing him told off, nobody could agree with her remarks. Everyone remained silent, even those who were opposed to him and considered that he had committed a great crime. They were ashamed to lift their heads, to look each other in the face, and for two reasons. Because Fabyash had sunk so low that he had stolen food from a child, and because Mrs Hudess, who was regarded as such a refined person, had burst forth with the language of the coarsest market vendor. To what depths suffering can bring a person.

Nevertheless no one spoke a word and Fabyash could have dug a grave and buried himself if his wife had not come to his aid. Fabyash's wife, who was ill and hardly able to move, her swollen hands and legs covered with chilblains in summer and winter, exploded. Although she was not allowed to move about or excite herself she could no longer watch her husband's humiliation. From where she stood, she poured forth, so that everyone turned to look, hardly knowing where the voice came from, 'Well, well! What an important matter! Just look at the Warsaw madam! A Warsaw lady indeed!' Without moving from the one spot, like a snowman that might fall to pieces at the slightest touch, her mouth crackled and sent forth fire and brimstone.

'Nothing is good enough for her. She wants the whole world. Her eyes are bigger than her stomach. In what way is your child better than mine? What if my hungry baby did take something in its mouth? The child is only skin and bones now. You can count his ribs. Here, just look.'

And Mrs Fabyash wasted no time in unfastening the child's shirt and she pointed out his thin bones, and pushed him towards Mrs Hudess. The boy, used to being ignored, was at first pleased that his mother was standing up for him and that he was the centre of attention. He grew up in his own eyes. But then he saw his mother's twisted face, the tears that welled in her throat and felt her hands stumbling over his thin body and he began to cry, his voice rising higher and higher. The child's tears gave his mother more courage and she really began on Mrs Hudess.

'You will not easily be forgiven this child's tears. God will punish you for this! So you really want to play the grand lady here. Just take a look at yourself! You are going about—you will pardon me—with the seat out of your pants. You look like a real beggar. You haven't got a decent stitch to your back. It's enough to make one scream with laughter, God help me.'

Then Mrs Fabyash began to laugh—she laughed bitterly and uncontrollably. She bent almost double with laughter, forgetting that so much movement was forbidden her and that she must not get agitated. The people who stood around became frightened and were afraid that she would collapse or that she had lost her reason. But she would allow no one near her and pushed everyone away. The blood drained from Mrs Hudess's face and she quivered. Furtively, she glanced at her clothes, which, in truth, were very worn, but no tear or hole was to be found. The few dresses that she owned were now falling to pieces but they were always cleanly washed and mended. She had not expected such an insult from Fabyash's wife.

Slowly and with much dignity she approached Mrs Fabyash and pushed her. She pushed her with the proud expression of one who strikes a person far below herself and repugnant to her. Nothing else was needed. Mrs Fabyash grabbed her by her blouse and both women were soon grappling together. Everything happened so quickly and so unexpectedly that they were already fighting before the men could tear them apart. The children's screams rose higher and some sailors who bore a grudge against the Jews, whom they blamed for having to remain at sea so long with new dangers to face every day, stood around in a circle jeering and laughing. In every crease and wrinkle of their leathery, wind-swept faces lurked the joy of seeing someone else hurt. In their eyes shone a malevolent insolence. They were bored and were looking for amusement to while away the hours. Now they had found the very thing and they incited the women against each other, shouting in their own language which no one understood and gesticulating wildly, adding fuel to the fire.

'Give her a good smack, mother! That's the way! Don't spare her. Harder still! We'll soon see who is the strongest.' The sailors almost spat into their hands with pleasure, delighted to see the Jews fighting amongst themselves.

'Now then, Jews, why do you stand with your hands in your pockets? Why do you let your wives do all the fighting?'

But the men did not become involved in the fight. On the contrary, they tried to pull the women apart. And when they had been separated and were ashamed that they had so far forgotten themselves, Reb Lazar, the grocer, pale and stony faced, was very angry with them.

'Fie!' he shouted without looking in their direction. 'You should be deeply ashamed of yourselves! What has happened here? Almighty God, this is even worse than when Christians get drunk. Who has ever seen Jews, and above all, women, fighting? This is the end of the world.'

Now everyone was on Fabyash's side, for they knew that Mrs Hudess began the fight. Fabyash now rode on a high horse. But his enemies couldn't stand the way he gave himself airs and wore such an innocent expression as if he couldn't put two and two together. They knew quite well that for some time Fabyash had furtively hoarded food, and in his suitcase there was quite a store, so that the rats had plenty to do there. More than once they had noticed him pull something secretly from his coat pocket and now the time had come for the bubble to burst.

And so that no time would be lost, his enemies pulled everyone into the cabin to his suitcase to see what was there.

After this, Fabyash went about as though he was not in this world. He avoided everyone and it was clear that something was happening to the young man who had once been so assertive and held such a high opinion of himself. He was no longer the same person. Reb Lazar, the grocer, who knew the Hebrew calendar backwards and always knew when it was the Sabbath and all the holy days, told the Jews when they assembled for prayer:

'It was wrong to shame Fabyash so.' He spoke half to the others and half into his own narrow, thin beard, freshly combed and bright for the Sabbath.

'A Jew doesn't steal. He took it innocently. And this shame will remain with him forever and ever. After all, what kind of a sin did he commit? In dire need even the Sabbath can be set aside. One has stronger nerves and can stand more. Another has weaker nerves and—may it never happen to us—breaks down. He'd had as much as he could take. In vain a Jew has been hurt. He may do something terrible to himself...'

In truth, Fabyash had broken down. On top of all this another calamity occurred which drove him to distraction. Why did this have to happen to him? He asked himself, shouted the question at his little girl.

In the middle of the day she had contracted a high temperature; her head ached and her legs gave way. Fabyash fell into a rage with himself and he could not forgive her as though she were to blame.

'Unlucky child, there is nothing the matter with you,' he vented his rage on the child when she complained that she was too tired to take another step.

'You're only talking yourself into it. You're only whining. It'll soon pass away. This would happen to me!'

He took no notice of the child's deep sighs, didn't want to hear anything or know anything, and he let his daughter walk around as if nothing had happened. He even warned her to say nothing to her mother, to keep quiet so that no one would get to know anything about it. Silently he took her hand, walked on to the deck and settled down there in a corner hoping that in the fresh air she would recover. And if anyone passed and asked why the child's cheeks were so flushed he would cut them short:

'There is nothing wrong with her. She's just had a bad turn. I'm sitting with her in the fresh air.'

But Fabyash couldn't conceal his child's illness for long. That night his daughter collapsed with a high fever and her whole body became covered in red spots. Then his wife attacked him, complaining bitterly that he had not said anything to her.

'Madman! Murderer!' she insulted him. 'What people say about you is only too true. When people call one a drunkard it is time to go to bed. Do you want to kill my child? You have a heart of stone! Save us, good people. Oh, my daughter! What is the matter with you?'

But Fabyash would not allow her to shout or to call to the others. He covered her mouth with his hand.

'Shh,' he pleaded with her. 'Perhaps by morning the fever will have gone. When people hear of it you and the child will be thrown out of here. Can't you understand that? Perhaps it is—God forbid—'

Fabyash did not complete the sentence. He was troubled and his arms hung limply by his side. But he didn't need to say it, for his wife had immediately understood what he meant. As if by a secret agreement they both remained silent, waiting to see what the morning would bring. But the morning brought no change. The child was no better. All night the mother had not closed her eyes. Like the child, she tossed and turned on the bed, constantly getting up in her nightgown to see how her daughter was getting on. After tossing all night in a fever the child fell asleep towards morning. Then she became delirious and every few minutes woke and screamed that someone was following her—that she was being chased and the ship was burning.

No matter how Fabyash tried to conceal the misfortune, in the morning everybody knew about it and discussed it fearfully.

'Fabyash's child has fallen ill. It can be nothing but typhus! Fabyash can't pull the wool over our eyes. We must see that something is done about it. The plague can easily spread. Job's sorrows have fallen on this Jew's head!'

They wanted to go to the captain and tell him everything; but they didn't do it for fear of hurting Fabyash. Meanwhile all those who had slept in the fetid, dirty, dark cabin with Fabyash moved out and settled elsewhere. Nobody even poked a nose into Fabyash's cabin except the distinguished Warsaw doctor who was constantly bustling about. He came with his instruments and the few medicines that he had rescued and guarded meticulously. And Bronya Feldbaum was not afraid. She, together with Mrs Fabyash, never left the child. Water was impossible to obtain except for the small quantity issued daily to each person that was hardly sufficient for an individual. Nevertheless Bronya brought a jug of water from somewhere and put cold compresses on the child. She carried out all the doctor's orders and was his right hand. When he examined the child and took her temperature she held her, soothed her with stories and was of great assistance to the mother.

The doctor was alive again. A new soul had entered into him. His thick, aristocratic moustache moved boldly up and down and his broad, black, artist's hat now sat proudly on his long hair that was the colour of tarnished silver. His eyes shone like one who had just regained his lost reputation. He constantly and reverently polished his instruments with a clean handkerchief which stood out white against his grubby clothing so that it drew every eye. Like a religious Jew he was always wetting his hands and rubbing them with soap. He didn't wipe them on the towel but held them in the air until they dried. He was so busy and excited that big drops of sweat appeared on his brow and he talked incessantly of cleanliness and hygiene, although he himself was far from clean.

But nothing went smoothly for the doctor, and he had great difficulty with the little girl who was shy in his presence and resisted him when he uncovered her and resolutely prevented him from properly examining her fever-ridden body. No matter how hard Bronya tried to distract her attention by telling her countless stories, she would not allow her body to be exposed when the doctor was near. The child cried and screamed and told the doctor to go away and when she was forcibly uncovered she struggled with her last ounce of energy and covered herself again. She would not allow them to cut off her thick, fair plaits and protected her head with her hands. Although the little girl often lost consciousness and talked deliriously she became lucid whenever Bronya approached her plaits with the scissors. She drove Bronya away and with tears in her eyes, dim with fever and the constantly burning electric light, she pleaded with her mother:

'Mama, where are you?' She looked about for her mother who had deliberately hidden herself so that she would not have to take part.

'I don't want my hair shorn. I don't want it, Mama!'

The doctor worked hard, moved his feet helplessly, continually wiped the sweat from his brow and held out his hands like one in despair. Nothing helped; the child remained obstinate and Fabyash had to come to the doctor's aid. Only when her father shouted at her in a strained voice did she take her hands from her head. As the thick fair plaits fell on to the bed like severed limbs the child gazed at them, unable to tear her tearful eyes away. She demanded the plaits to play with, not wanting to let them out of her hands. It was only with difficulty that her mother succeeded in taking the hair away from her. She had to persuade her that when she was well she would get her plaits back.

The doctor did not spare himself and never left the child, night or day. But it was all in vain—there was no improvement. Everyone on the ship knew that Fabyash's daughter had typhus. His boy had long since been taken away from Fabyash and he slept elsewhere. Everyone went about in great fear that the typhus would spread throughout the ship. They thought the best thing to do would be to disclose everything to the captain. But nobody wanted to do it and each was afraid to give voice to his thoughts. The first to speak out was Reb Zainval Rockman. The self-assertive Zainval Rockman never lost his head and he said emphatically and openly that it was time the captain was told what was happening. But he saw that no one wanted to make a move and that he would have to do it himself. In his slow, measured voice he said that of course he would be called an informer, but if saving a ship full of Jews was inform-ing then he would be an informer and gladly carry that sin on his own shoulders.

Whether Zainval Rockman went to the captain or not was never discovered. But on the very day when he spoke so emphatically, two sailors with a senior officer, a doctor, appeared at Fabyash's cabin.

Fabyash's wife, more dead than alive, pleaded with the officer not to take away her child. She vowed there was nothing wrong with her; she had only caught a chill and was running a slight temperature. But it was to no avail. The officer, a short, stout, well-groomed man scarcely even looked at her. He didn't examine the child, but cast one glance at her and, in his own language, angrily ordered the sailors to use the stretcher they had prepared. Mrs Fabyash called the Greek who was travelling with them, thinking that he might soften the heart of the officer, but he also failed. Then Mrs Fabyash, in her misery, signed to her husband not to stand like a dummy and stare foolishly, but to do something. But Fabyash stood by helplessly, hardly moving from his place. Mrs Fabyash seized the officer by his sleeve and clung to him.

'Your honour! Herr! Doctor! Panya!' she implored him in Polish. 'Have pity in your heart! Don't take from me my joy. Your honour! Herr! I have only two small children.'

The officer didn't even look at her, nor did he understand one word she said. He tore his sleeve away and brushed it as if an ugly insect had crawled on it. Mrs Fabyash turned her back and fumbled with her trembling hands at her blouse. She pulled out a small brooch set with tiny stones and offered it to the officer, saying in Polish:

'Take the brooch Your Honour! Doctor! This is all I possess. I saved this brooch for a black hour. Now the black hour has come! Take it Panya.'

The officer greedily took the brooch and examined it carefully and expertly to see how much it was worth, debating with himself whether he should take it; but in the end he gave it back.

Meanwhile the sailors had picked up the child, who did not open her tired eyes, and placed her on the stretcher. Mrs Fabyash stood in the doorway with her arms outstretched like wings and would not let them go out.

'I will stand here,' she said with great determination, 'I will not allow you out of here! Only over my dead body!'

She was so roughly shoved aside that she fell to the floor, and the sailors took the stretcher away.

Many people had assembled near the door and they sympathised with Mrs Fabyash. The first to step forward were Nathan and Noah, 'the red', Bronya's brother.

'Be more careful!' Nathan said. 'Don't push. Is that the way to treat passengers?'

The sailors looked him up and down as if they couldn't understand how this young man had so much cheek and then burst into a loud laugh.

'Passengers? What kind of passengers are you? A band of tramps, that's what you are! Dirty Jews!' called the smaller sailor with the scar on his face. He was broad shouldered and nearly black from the sun, with strong hands, on one of which was tattooed a naked dancer with long, slender legs.

Nathan's blood drained from his face, his grey eyes became pale and his lips trembled. He wanted to speak out against the sailor but words failed him and a lump stuck in his throat. Noah came to his aid and he spoke more with his hands than his mouth, more in Yiddish than in Greek.

'Take those words back!' He forced the words out and his black, curly hair fell over his face while his eyes burnt with hatred. He was ready to attack anyone who stood against him.

'Take those words back! We will not allow ourselves to be trampled in the mud. We demand decent treatment! We are human beings!'

The taller sailor with a head of black hair, a rolling gait, and an Adam's apple than ran up and down his throat like a mouse angrily taunted Noah. 'Human beings? Important people! You have been thrown out of everywhere and no one will take you in. All doors and gates are closed to you. We can't put in at any port because of you. Everybody is afraid you'll get your feet in and will never go away.'

The Jews held back Noah who had quite lost control of himself. Everyone began to shout at the sailors, especially at the officer, whom they blamed for the trouble. Although no one had completely understood what the sailor had said, the few words they had followed had hurt them deeply enough. With one voice they shouted in Yiddish:

'Don't insult passengers! Watch your words!'

'It's a shame to say such things!'

'Treat us like human beings, not like dogs! Even dogs are treated better.'

'We want food. You eat and drink but we haven't seen a piece of bread. And as for meat, that's out of the question! The stew makes us sick and sticks to our teeth like tar. We can't put it in our mouths: it's a shame!'

Hearing the word 'food', Marcus Feldbaum, 'the ox', stood forth and beat his breast with his powerful fists till it almost echoed.

'We want food!' he shouted. 'We are hungry! You are starving the passengers! The world is not all wild and barbarous!'

When the sailors saw that it was no longer a laughing matter, that the group was growing bigger, they grabbed the stretcher and left. But they still had the last word, for as they were going they shouted back:

'You eat for nothing! Dirty Jews!'

When the sailors had gone Fabyash looked around and saw that the brooch was missing. He thought that his wife, who had followed the stretcher, must have hidden it. But she knew nothing of it.

Soon the doctor and one of the sailors returned to Fabyash's cabin. The sailor threw Fabyash's suitcase outside and sprayed the cabin with a disinfectant and nailed up the door. Fabyash and his family, together with the suitcase, were led away like convicts.

A little later, when calm had descended on the ship, the Warsaw doctor was seen to walk in the direction of the captain's cabin with dignified, assured steps, his black, artist's hat pulled low down on his forehead. No one knew where he was going or what had suddenly occurred to him. But soon everything was clear, for from the captain's cabin came shouts. Stealing up to the door, they heard the doctor banging on the table and angrily demanding that he be allowed to see the sick child. He had begun the treatment and demanded to continue to attend to her. He had a right to do that. He had forty years' practice behind him. He was no mere boy.

But all his anger and his banging on the table didn't help him—he was not permitted to enter the ship's hospital. He left the captain with his head bowed in humiliation. As much as he had been proud and dignified in approaching the captain so he was now dejected and pathetic. He could barely move his legs as he muttered to himself:

'Forty years' practice behind me! Forty years! So many sick have passed through my hands. What has happened to you, Doctor Bronislaw Mirsky?'

He stopped and threw his instruments on the deck and pushed them with his feet as though they were worthless things. But soon he picked them up, dusted them, and went on his way.

Late after lunch Fabyash and his family returned from the disinfecting room. His head was shaved and his clothes rumpled and covered with yellow stains. He looked as if he had just returned from prison. His wife's head was shaven and covered with tufts of hair like a little boy's. She looked like a boy, younger by half her years. She smiled foolishly and was very shy but her shame was soon hidden by a scarf.

The rumour spread that all those who had slept on the lower deck with Fabyash would have to be disinfected. Certainly several sailors had come with him, searched the cabins, looked under the bunks, examined every corner and written something in a notebook. Furiously they shouted names and ordered everyone to line up. The sailors drove everyone along, warning that no one must fall out or hide because time was short—it would soon be nightfall.

The Jews became frightened, fell in line and allowed themselves to be driven like a flock of sheep. Each one carried his possessions, a tattered suitcase or a bundle, and it looked as though they were going on a long journey. Everyone obeyed the sailors meekly except Bronya Feldbaum, who paced restlessly up and down and shouted that she was not filthy and she would not stand the shame of being dragged off to the disinfecting room like the worst vagrant. In addition, she would not allow them to cut off her hair, she would prefer to jump into the water and take her own life rather than submit to such shame. Meanwhile she covered her head with her hands just like Fabyash's little girl had. Then she broke away from the others and disappeared for a while. She returned with a triumphant and secretive gleam in her tear-stained, swollen, red eyes. But she couldn't keep her secret for long. With a wink she told the others that only those women who were quite clean would keep their hair; the scissors would just be run over them.

Amongst those taken to the disinfecting room was Ida, who stood with her head erect and did not reply to Nathan's encouraging glance. Nathan waited for her to return and when she came back with her hair trimmed he joked with her and said that she looked prettier than before. The boyish haircut went well with her thick, husky voice and her obstinate manner.

'You look just like a cheeky boy,' and he kissed her hastily clipped hair, 'a naughty little urchin. It suits you very well.'

But all the work was of no avail, for that night Reb Lazar's wife and his son, with the long side curls pushed behind his ears and the traditional cap on his head, both fell ill. And Reb Lazar immediately notified the crew and his family was removed to the hospital.

CHAPTER VI

On the following night, while the Warsaw doctor was fast asleep, someone knocked on his door and woke him. In the murky darkness the doctor could see nothing, but he felt a pair of hands pulling at him to call him to a sick person. The doctor trembled with excitement and he could not find his clothes. Not listening to the whispering voice, he followed blindly with his shirt unbuttoned. Obediently he followed a figure through the darkness up and down steps, through side passages, and heard about a sailor who had suddenly become ill.

The doctor strained to catch the strange words in the darkness and asked about the sailor's condition. He was once again full of courage and a renewed

belief in himself, and he was determined to do everything in his power to save the sick person. He would
show everybody who Doctor Bronislaw Mirsky was!

With a thumping heart the doctor entered the
sick man's cabin. His anxious eyes wandered over
the walls and the faces of the sailors who sat around;
but he learnt nothing. He searched for the sick man
and found him lying in a bunk. He walked over to
him, sat down by his side and smelt the alcohol and
cheap tobacco that pervaded the cabin. He was in
command, and with confidence he began to order
the sailors about, gesturing with his hands as to
the deaf, scolding them for not looking after the
sick person, for leaving him in such a stifling
atmosphere where one could hardly breathe. Then
he gently patted the sick man and went to work. But
no sooner had he put the stethoscope on the patient's
chest than the sick man stood up, stretched himself
to his full height, and exploded with laughter right in
the doctor's face. The doctor's expression changed
rapidly in fright and bewilderment and twisted as if
from sudden paralysis. All the sailors who had been
sitting with serious faces burst out laughing. They
were bent double and their uproarious shouts echoed
in the stillness of the night. Cushions and other
articles flew at the doctor's head.

The doctor kept this a great secret, burying it all deep within himself. The Jews discovered it from the sailors themselves who constantly boasted about how they had fooled the distinguished doctor. The insult stirred everyone deeply and they were overcome with indignation. Although more than once they themselves had laughed at the half-senile old doctor and made jokes at his expense, this hoax was more than they could bear. Each one felt the insult personally, and their misery was deepened because Fabyash's little son had been removed to the hospital and the disease had not spared his neighbour, a healthy, tall young man, nor the deaf Greek passenger's wife. The whole ship smelt of carbolic. Of the fate of the sick no one knew anything. Mrs Fabyash ran several times a day to the ship's hospital on her swollen legs, but she was never allowed inside. She had forgotten that she was not allowed to exert herself and the swelling of her legs and hands was growing worse. She hung around the hospital door and more than once she almost got inside; but she was always pushed out and sent away.

Reb Lazar remained calm and went about as if nothing had happened. This irritated Fabyash and he muttered angrily to himself:

'He's neither a man nor a father.'

He could not understand Reb Lazar's behaviour, for it appeared that he was not worried at all.

'He has a parched heart like a bandit! What's the use of his praying all day?'

The Jews could not remain silent about the story of the doctor's humiliation or about the insults of the sailors when they removed Fabyash's little daughter to hospital, and they decided to go and complain to the captain. People shouldn't be trodden underfoot; the world isn't altogether lawless! If we allow ourselves to be trodden on things will only get worse. Something must be done about it!

They assembled in Rockman's cabin. The chairman was Zainval Rockman himself, who still held his head high. He suffered from nothing so much as the absence of cigarettes. He was a heavy smoker and his hands and his small shovel-like beard, which he was always stroking, were still stained with nicotine. He could readily have dispensed with food and water for the sake of a cigarette which would have calmed his nerves. From habit Rockman produced the silver cigarette case which was the only relic from his regally furnished three rooms and a kitchen; but he found nothing in it. His eyes always searched the floor and on more than one occasion he was tempted to pick up the cigarette butts the sailors had thrown

away, but at the last moment he had restrained
himself. He had no money to bribe the sailors with
and he hadn't the heart to give away the cigarette
case, the last of his belongings and the only souvenir
of his engagement to the young wife who had died
soon after their marriage. How would he have looked
in the eyes of his daughter, now a grown-up woman?
And he couldn't lower himself to ask for a cigarette. Reb Zainval Rockman was not in the habit
of holding out his hand; he was more accustomed
to giving. He who was accustomed to giving away
cigarettes wouldn't ask for one—especially as he was
afraid of a refusal.

The Jews who had assembled in Rockman's cabin
decided to go to the captain and demand to be told
what had happened to the sick: if they were being
treated or just lying in the hospital like dogs. Things
must not be allowed to drift. They could not wait any
longer. Every day things were getting worse! They
could not remain silent!

But there was no one to go. Who would be able
to explain what they wanted, to use a strong word
where necessary? Someone suitable would have to be
chosen, or perhaps two, to defend the insulted Jews.

Soon it became clear that there was nothing
to worry about, for Nathan and Noah were both

anxious to go. Nathan said he knew something of the Greek language and he would be able to speak up.

So away they went. The captain did not receive them immediately, saying he would have some spare time later in the day. They waited impatiently and when they finally appeared before the captain they found that he did not seem to be as bad a man as had been thought. To tell the truth, he was very nervous, sickly and silent. He fidgeted on his chair; to every ten words he answered with one; he glanced continually at his wrist-watch and kept brushing with his hand the captain's cap that lay on the table. Every few minutes he got up and, from beneath his stiff, unruly eyebrows like birds' nests, he gazed around the poorly furnished cabin. On the small, plain table lay untidy writing materials and a photograph of a woman. A battered cupboard, a few chairs and an old map which almost covered one wall, completed the furnishings.

The captain barely understood what Nathan was saying and screwed up his thin, long face as if wanting to help him squeeze out the words that lay so heavily on his tongue. In the end the captain made out what it was he wanted to say and he became pale, as anger spread from his thin, determined lips to his sharply marked sideboards. But he controlled himself and smilingly promised that he would do whatever lay in his power to see that the passengers should have nothing more to complain of.

But the good work was wasted, for only a few hours after Nathan and Noah returned with the good tidings, a sailor attacked Bronya Feldbaum and dragged her into a corner out of sight of everybody. The sailor was short and very broad, with strangely long, gnarled arms that projected from his short-sleeved, dirty shirt like twisted roots. His arms were so long that they almost reached to the ground and they were as strong as they were long. He grabbed Bronya in these arms as in an iron vice, at the same time glancing meaningfully at his bulging pockets. His lips were wet and pouting and he breathed out burning words.

'I have a tin of sardines. You're beautiful,' he whispered passionately, and his small eyes narrowed and became dull like faded beads.

'A full tin! They would give me a fortune for it but I won't take it. I kept it for my beauty—to make my sweet pigeon look even better. And I've got something else here. Come with me and I will show you. Come! Over there no one will see us.'

The sailor said much more to Bronya, explaining with his hands to make sure she would understand him. He pointed to and winked at his stuffed pockets as if great treasure was hidden there, and poured out affectionate and lewd words. He pointed boastfully to himself and said that he was a real man and that she was his chosen one. She was not to worry that he was so ugly. He emptied his pockets at her feet and rapidly pleaded in his own language, forgetting that she could not understand a word.

'Here! Take everything I've got.'

He pressed her to his heavy body.

'I can't sleep at night because of you. You have robbed me of my sleep, my beautiful one, my sweet one.'

Bronya was revolted by the sailor and was afraid that someone might overhear. She knew him. He was very hardworking and often did the work of others, so that the sailors made jokes at his expense and treated him as a fool. Bronya pleaded with him with tears in her eyes, and struggled with him till she was exhausted. Suddenly she became possessed of such strength that with one shove she pushed him away from her so that he staggered and almost fell backwards.

His eyes blazed craftily to warn her that he knew she was no innocent girl and he winked insolently to imply that he was not one of those fools who could be fobbed off with nothing.

'I want to enjoy myself too,' he tittered. 'Why shouldn't I? In what way is the steward you knock around with at night better than me? Is it because he's handsome? He's got the face of a doll. They've got their eyes on him, don't worry. He won't steal any more of those delicacies for you. They're watching that thief all right. You'll die of hunger now. Who'll give you nice things to keep your body beautiful?'

The sailor moved slowly towards her, looking for an opportunity to hurl himself at her. But she watched every movement and gesture of his powerful body, moving back all the time. Suddenly she slipped away from him and began to run. She ran as if from a fire, through many passages, panting, certain that he was following her. With her last ounce of strength she burst into her husband's cabin, and threw herself into his arms and clung to his big body as though afraid somebody might tear her away. She caressed him, held him tightly as if to seek shelter from her misfortune. Marcus did not know what could have happened to his wife and tried to soothe her. But still she clung to him without speaking. At length she burst into tears and began to complain.

'Why do you always leave me alone? I have a

husband. Why aren't you like other men who look after their wives? Won't you be nice to me? You won't leave me again, will you?'

Her husband wanted to know what had happened but she would not say anything. But Bronya was recovering and later, when she went to bed, she could no longer keep it to herself. She got hold of Ida and cried, telling her that only an intelligent person like her could understand. Bronya knew that Ida had gone to secondary school and matriculated. And she too had been to secondary school.

Bronya told Ida everything. All her former reserve had vanished and she didn't care that she was waking up everybody in the cabin. It made no difference when Ida tried to quieten her and stroked her still fresh, full cheeks and her thick hair that had been cut short at the time of the disinfection. Ida whispered into her ear that everybody was awake and listening to every word and begged her to talk more quietly. But Bronya took no notice.

'Why did this have to happen to me?' she complained loudly. 'What have I done to deserve it? It makes me sick even now. It is revolting to think of such a thing.'

The other women had been awakened by Bronya's sobs. They recognised her voice and instantly pricked up their ears. In the darkness voices arose, although no faces were to be seen. Darkness covered everything as with a black curtain and voices fell upon Bronya and mercilessly flayed her.

'What is she crying for? What is all the fuss about? When she sees a pair of pants she swoons! Why does she play the role of a wounded innocent?'

'Why is it that nobody touches me, only her?' somebody asked in a cracked, old voice, that became shrill with anger. 'I don't play around with everybody. I don't run around at night so no one treats me insolently. It serves you right. Who tells you to go where you're not supposed to? A Galician lady to behave so foolishly!'

'Oh, how terrible! Someone touched the crown of the nun's head. She had never seen a man before in all her life,' a self-righteous voice from afar rose above the other women.

'We don't sell ourselves. You would think we had more to eat than she had!'

Bronya had never expected such a reception. She became silent, and tried with all her strength to keep back her tears. She stuffed her fists into her mouth so that not even a whimper should escape. But it did not work. The things she had heard had stripped her and she felt she could not bear it. A pain shot through her heart and she sobbed quietly as she lay in Ida's arms. The tears rolled down her cheeks and she answered nothing. She submitted to her punishment, feeling a load lifted from her heart. She wanted the talk to continue. She was guilty and she was paying the penalty.

And the women went on talking without a pause. The beds creaked with malice and the women took revenge on Bronya for everything that had happened. Nobody could be distinguished in the darkness and each one let her tongue run freely and said just what she wanted to.

CHAPTER VII

The next day the women had something to tell the men. And even Ida couldn't restrain herself from telling Nathan. She confessed that she wasn't any better than the other women; she was just a woman with a loose tongue and liked to gossip just as they did. She called herself an idle chatterer and, with childish charm, slapped her own face. Nevertheless she told Nathan everything, dotting all the i's. She enjoyed the piquant situation and rattled on in her husky voice.

Nathan didn't take it as lightly as Ida had. It worried him greatly that all his representations to the captain had helped only as much as a plaster on a dead man and that Bronya had been so insulted. He

felt it deeply as evidence of a contemptuous attitude
to all the Jews on the ship. He told Ida, but she was
so cheerful and lighthearted that she paid no attention to his talk and ironically called him 'preacher'
and 'fighter'.

'The sea looks so beautiful,' she said with a child-
ish gesture and she wrinkled her impudent, snub
nose, screwed up her amber eyes and showed her
straight, white teeth.

'Look at your serious face. You've become a real
fighter lately! You hardly ever look at me. See how
beautiful everything is!'

It really was a beautiful, sunny morning, although
it was very hot. The water was smooth and so crystal
clear that one could look deep into the bed of the
sea. The sun had just risen, washed by the clean blue
waters, and still retained the purity of the newly born
as it tinted the sky around with gold. A little warm
wind touched the surface of the water and gently
rippled it without disturbing the great calm which
lay over God's earth.

Ida and Nathan strolled the deck. She took his
arm but he could not forget her reproach and he
scarcely glanced at her. But Ida radiated energy and
vitality and soon he began to feel more certain of
himself, like a child near its mother. He felt her hand

under his arm and all his old dreams began to stir in him again. Of these he had many; they changed from day to day and often had no basis. Plans that he had played with for a day now assumed some reality and appeared possible to realise. He walked beside Ida full of schemes, worked out to the last detail, of what he would do in the new land whither they were bound. He would resume his studies and finish his engineering course. This was a profession that was in demand everywhere. In every country in the world an engineer could make a living and feel firm earth beneath his feet. He had had enough of business. He was not cut out for that. After every few words he would ask Ida if she understood him and if she agreed with him. For him only one thing was necessary—to begin his studies again. Not for nothing had his old father had so much faith in him and been certain that he would grow up to be something. When as a student he had come home to the little township, his father, a timid and self-effacing man, had taken him along to the synagogue and prided himself before the leading citizens on his talented son. The heart of the poor artisan swelled with joy when the eminent Jews from the front benches honoured him by paying attention to his son, questioning him about Warsaw, good humouredly inquiring whether the city still stood in the same place.

And later at dinner the door had been never still. Through it came a stream of cakes and puddings borne by the shy girls of the township who were too bashful to look in Nathan's direction but mumbled through their noses to his father and mother, 'A welcome to your guest.'

A rich match was proposed for him, but he was not interested in it, preferring to use his spare time to devour every book that came to his hand. His aloofness hurt his father, who wanted him to talk to people. But Nathan, who could not stand his father's humility and his anxiety for the future of his gifted son, never gave him that satisfaction. He saw something of his father in himself, so he never stayed long in the township, always hurrying to return to the city.

But where did all this lead? He had never achieved anything, because he never had any money. He had not been admitted to any faculty at the university. He had had no chance of going abroad although he had always dreamed of travelling. His life never proceeded smoothly. He worked beyond his strength, teaching and studying far into the night by a kerosene lamp in poor boarding houses. While he studied he bit his nails until it hurt, stubbornly pursuing the road he had chosen and having no time for anything else. Although he had disliked the way his father had wanted to make him the light of his poor life, sacrificing his last bite for him, he hadn't departed far from his father's path. He had gone against his father deliberately, always quarrelling with him, though he had always wanted to realise the same dreams—but it hadn't worked.

Nathan and Ida stood near the rails of the deck as they talked and did not notice that Zainval Rockman and Noah, 'the red', stood near by. Rockman had been searching since early morning for someone to tell his stories to, slowly and with a voice full of dignity. All the time he had been on the ship anxiety had built up within him and he was pining to get it off his chest. He was aching to talk just as he ached for a cigarette. At home he had loved to preside over the table, taking a leading role. But on the ship he no longer shone; he drifted about like a discarded rag; nobody noticed him and nobody listened to him. His white, starched collar was no longer spotless as it had always been and his well-trimmed, shovel-shaped beard was untidy and neglected. He didn't play the part he should amongst such a congregation of Jews. Although he was often annoyed with the way Fabyash always knew more than everyone else and would not listen to the few but inspired words from the mouth of Zainval Rockman himself—words that were stretched out to give them their full value—it was precisely to Fabyash that he loved to talk. He liked to argue with him and to prove him an ignoramus who knew nothing. But since Fabyash's sorrows had caused him to roam the ship distractedly Rockman had no one to talk to and he went about with the young people. He is not old-fashioned, he is not conservative, he reads newspapers and books and knows what is going on in the world. He talked to the young people with carefully chosen words learned from the newspapers and from his two sons. They were words he did not use well.

Although Zainval Rockman liked best to talk himself he would politely listen to others. But what they said was of no importance; it went in one ear and out the other. He waited for the other person to finish, meanwhile thinking out what he was going to say next and smiling at the great thought that had occurred to him and the clever words that lay on the tip of his tongue. He listened to Noah with pretended patience as Noah complained that he was on the ship only because of his brother-in-law, Marcus Feldbaum, and cursed the day that brought him there. He could now be in Russia, not only in Russia, but in his own city Lvov, where Soviet power ruled and the Red Flag flew over the town hall. All his life he had fought in Lvov and been imprisoned in all its gaols in the struggle for the emancipation of the workers and now that victory had come he had to be far away and unable to see it with his own eyes.

'Do you know what joy it gives me,' Noah said more to Nathan and Ida than to Rockman; 'In my own Lvov, the hammer and sickle flies freely and proudly over the town hall! Lvov was always a city of struggle. It produced Botwin, one of our own. He was a good comrade and a hero. His name has been enshrined in the history of the working class.'

Noah's eyes flashed and his black curly hair shook as he talked as though to himself.

'The revolutionary songs ring out clearly and freely in the workers' clubs and trade unions in Lvov and I am here! And all because of my brother-in-law. He was always friendly, a good brother, although he was rich. He treated the peasants well, worked together with them. But, forgive me for saying so, he was always a big ox. The best proof is that he has always allowed my sister to lead him by the nose.'

And Noah told how Marcus always had a plan to go to Palestine and settle on the land there. But he, Noah, had persuaded him to go to Biro-Bidjan.

In the end he hadn't gone anywhere, because his wife, the Parisian dame, wouldn't allow him to go. So when the war broke out and Germany seized almost the whole of Poland, his brother-in-law had harnessed a peasant wagon, and, with everything he could save, was convinced that he was going to Palestine at last. Meanwhile he went to Rumania, and he took Noah with him.

But he didn't get to Palestine because he wasn't allowed to enter. He no more went to Palestine than Noah had gone back to Lvov, although he had tried hard enough when he heard that the Red Army had entered that city. The refugees with whom he had wandered through many countries had always pushed him on, never allowing him to turn back. They had talked him down and told him that no one was ever allowed to enter Russia, until he became confused and didn't know where he was.

Rockman listened to Noah, barely restraining himself from interrupting. Something lay on the tip of his tongue, something that would show the young people that he was not a stick in the mud, that he had his eyes open and knew what was going on around him. He wanted everyone to listen carefully to him and several times he coughed to add significance to what he was about to say. Gravely he began to tell of his two sons who had fought each other so often that he wanted to send them to the devil. He had often asked the younger one why the government didn't suit him. Why did he want to turn Poland upside down, legs up, head down? And the elder he had asked, why had he to go to Palestine? Why didn't Poland suit him?

But it appeared that his socially conscious sons—well educated young men with the brains of professors—were not so mad after all. They knew what they were talking about. He was convinced of that when high taxes choked him, stripped him as naked as Adam. He was not lazy and he went up to the taxation office to have a talk with the officials, to appeal to their conscience, to ask them why they wanted to strip him.

'I went to the office,' Zainval Rockman slowly measured out the words and stroked his beard as was his habit, 'dressed in the very best coat I possessed, not humbling myself as many of our brethren do, and went straight to the head. I always like to go to the head, not to the tail, if you will excuse the expression. And I asked the head "Why? Why precisely do you want to make a pauper of me?" Now guess what the gentile, that nobody of nobodies, answered me: "To get rid of you from Poland. If you don't like it you can go! It is high time the Jews left Poland."'

Reb Zainval coughed and looked around to see what effect his words had on his listeners. He was greatly excited, as if he was living through everything again. He continued to talk: 'What I lived through then! I wish my sufferings on Hitler, may his name be erased from history! I felt suffocated and I thought I would not be able to bear it. That I was being tossed around like a ball was no small thing! I was being thrown out and it seemed the world was coming to an end. And from then on I began to look at my brave sons with different eyes. When my eldest son left for Palestine I saw him off myself from Warsaw. Jews must have somewhere to rest their heads. My heart swelled with joy when I saw the young people dance on the station. What do you call that dance? Hora? And when some larrikin— a nobody, not really grown out of his nappies, but barking like someone of great importance—began to throw stones at the young people, I nearly broke his ribs. Disgraceful insolence! Imagine such a one lifting his hand!'

Zainval talked on and because he was being listened to, he never grew tired. Now he had the opportunity to pour it all out.

'Yes, since the affair with the taxes,' he went on,

'I felt that we, the handful of Jews, were without any protection. We are always on shifting sand and we need firm ground under our feet. A support and an ideal.'

His eyes shone with pleasure because of all the fine words he had spoken.

'Now, take for instance, the grocer! That slovenly Hassid has a support. Once I used to look at such Jews with contempt, holding that they made themselves and others mad. But now I can see that I made a mistake. Who can compare himself with Reb Lazar? Who is as well off as he is? We must know exactly where we are in this world. We must be either faithful to God or to man!'

Rockman had now really got into his stride and he would have talked and talked had not Ida pulled Nathan away. It was such a nice day, she said, and her head was already full of these sorrows. She was in a good mood and she wanted to go for a stroll.

CHAPTER VIII

Ever since Fabyash's two children had been taken to the hospital Mrs Hudess had somehow felt guilty. She couldn't look Mrs Fabyash in the eye and she sought an opportunity to make friends with her again. Her conscience troubled her, not giving her a moment's peace: she imagined that she was not guiltless, that her hand had played a part in the misfortune that had fallen on Mrs Fabyash. Besides, she was afraid for her own children, terrified that they might catch the infection.

The epidemic still raged and not one day passed without a new case. Everybody crept about carefully, as if they were afraid to touch the floor. They listened suspiciously to the merest sounds within themselves and every time something hurt or ached they were afraid.

Mrs Hudess anxiously watched over her children, not allowing them to play on the deck. Most of the time she kept the little girls locked in the cabin under her own eye and when they were out she went everywhere with them. But whenever she and the children passed Mrs Fabyash, her heart contracted and she felt guilty that her children were so bright and healthy while the other's lay seriously ill in the hospital. She covered her children up; she didn't want them to look so well. She wanted to disguise them, to make them smaller, so that they wouldn't be too conspicuous in Mrs Fabyash's eyes, so that the sight of them would not hurt her.

But she was mistaken. Mrs Fabyash didn't look with any bitterness upon the children, nor did she harbour any hatred. On the contrary she was delighted that the girls—may no evil eye light upon them—were in good health. Once when Mrs Hudess sidled past her, Mrs Fabyash stopped her, and, not looking in her direction, said, 'How are your daughters?' She spoke calmly as if nothing had happened between them. 'How are they getting on?'

Mrs Hudess trembled as if she were caught in a theft. She was terribly ashamed that she had harboured such ugly thoughts when the other woman was so good and so free from evil. It happened so quickly and unexpectedly that she was confused and didn't know what to answer. She lowered her head and stammered, speaking respectfully, 'How do I know?' She didn't know what she was going to say next and she had nothing to catch hold of. 'How do I know? How are you? How is your health?'

She only asked after Mrs Fabyash's health, afraid to remind her of the sick children. Mrs Fabyash saw through her embarrassment and evasions, and said, 'I can see that you're not feeling well.' She spoke solemnly so that this would sound more like an important occasion. 'I can see that you are hiding the children from me. Do you think I don't notice? But listen to what I have to say to you. Sweet Father in Heaven, may it happen to my children what I wish for yours! Let them at least be well. Is it their fault that such a misfortune has happened to me? I am not one of those mothers who live for revenge on others. God be with you.'

Tears welled in Mrs Fabyash's eyes and she wiped them away with her sleeve. Then she patted Mrs Hudess's little girls on their heads and murmured, 'Now go on with good health. Don't be worried. Have a walk with the children in the fresh air.'

But Mrs Hudess didn't go; she stood as if nailed to
the spot. Mrs Fabyash was the first to leave, shuffling
heavily away on her ailing legs which were covered
with chilblains and other swellings. Although she
was young she was very sick. She no longer wore a
scarf to cover her close-cropped hair, shorn like a
boy's during the disinfecting process. She was no
longer concerned about her appearance. Her young,
child-like head sat strangely on her bowed shoulders above her swollen flabby figure. It looked badly
matched, as though it had just been fitted on. It was
obvious that walking was difficult for her, that it cost
her great effort.

Mrs Hudess watched her for a long time and
turned her back to her children so that they wouldn't
see the tears that ran down her face. Then she slowly
went away. The children didn't allow her to stand
still and think for long. They were drawn to the
other children playing on the deck, but their mother
would not let them go there for fear of them catching the infection. Mrs Hudess deliberately walked
with her children to keep them from running about
too freely. But still the little girls longed to be with
those on deck or at least to watch them play, even
from a distance. So Mrs Hudess had no choice
but to give in and let them stand and watch from

a distance the other children at play.

Mrs Hudess stood absorbed in her sorrows and watched the children run about shouting and screaming. They were so immersed in their play that they didn't notice what was going on around them. Nor did they remember that they had had nothing in their mouths since morning. Their dirty hands and bare feet, emaciated and as thin as sticks that might easily break, moved quickly and nimbly. It is amazing where these urchins, with their match-like arms and legs, get the strength and energy to run around so much. Mrs Hudess stared at the playing children and kept an eye on her own little girls but her mind was somewhere else. Since her meeting with Mrs Fabyash she hadn't felt well, not nearly as well as she had before. She saw herself humbled. Instead of her asking for forgiveness, Mrs Fabyash had made overtures to her and really humiliated her. Mrs Fabyash had appeared so noble and refined and she, Mrs Hudess, looked so small and disclosed all her foolishness. She had come out of the encounter like a pricked balloon.

Mrs Hudess tortured herself with her reproaches that became stronger as she watched the youngsters turning everything upside down. She noticed a small girl approach the group of children. In her hand she held a white bread roll which some sailor, who had taken pity on her, must have given her. To the children who hadn't seen such a thing for weeks the piece of baked dough gleamed so white that it must have come from fairyland. They were drawn to it and they stopped their play and circled around the child with the roll like moths round a lamp at night. They drew nearer and nearer, stretching out their hands and begging for a little piece. The child broke off crumbs with a mean little hand and distributed them amongst the outstretched hands. Her eyes shone with pleasure and she was full of self-importance. She played the role of a patron, pinching off tiny pieces with two fingers. But the children demanded more and more. Then she noticed that there was hardly anything left in her hand, and she didn't want to give anyone any more. Helplessly she sat down on the floor and clutched to herself, with both hands, the remains of the roll. Then the others fell upon her, tore the piece of roll out of her hands and quickly disappeared.

Mrs Hudess watched all this and her self-accusations became more insistent. Why had she attacked Fabyash? How had it profited her? Fabyash had troubles enough.

Then on Friday, at midday when the sun was ripe

and full like a great golden pear that hung heavily from the centre of the sky, the captain called Nathan to him and announced that Fabyash's little daughter and the wife of Reb Lazar, the grocer, had died and the funeral would take place very shortly. Nobody would be allowed to go near the bodies but they could watch from a distance as they were lowered into the water to their eternal rest.

Nathan knew how the news would affect everybody and he stood pale and speechless, afraid to say anything. But they could read in his face that it was not good news he brought. And before he could open his mouth everybody knew what had happened. Death had flown in through the golden atmosphere, darkly hovering over every head. It came with the hot wind that whipped up the waves, driving them into one knot like sheep before a storm. Although everyone had known that the days of the sick were numbered and that at any moment some body might draw its last breath, no one had permitted himself to entertain that thought and each one hoped that the sick, with God's aid, would be restored to health.

When the bad news, that everybody had been waiting for with throbbing hearts, actually came, they were terrified, as if something unexpected had happened. They felt that death had touched each

one and threatened every family. Who knows how
long one can carry the disease around inside oneself
without knowing anything about it? Who knows
whose turn will be next?

Everybody came to the funeral. They pressed
close together in one corner as if each wanted to
feel the presence of his living neighbour—to inhale
his living breath and odour. The Warsaw doctor
came with his small, thin wife who nestled close to
him and held him firmly by his arm. Accustomed
back home to follow the gentile-style funerals of his
relatives without his hat, here he also respectfully
removed his broad-brimmed black hat. The wind
ruffled his long, neglected hair that was the colour
of old darkened silver. Ever since the sailors had so
deeply humiliated him he rarely talked, keeping the
insult buried within him, certain that no one knew
anything about it. And the Greek, whose wife had
been taken to the hospital, stood bareheaded also.
Noah stood uncertainly not knowing what to do,
holding his old, greasy, crumpled cap in his hands
but in the end putting it on. He always went hatless,
even for most of the winter, and he wore an open-
necked shirt so that the cap looked strange on him
and sat on the top of his head as if it didn't belong
to him.

Mrs Hudess and Bronya supported Mrs Fabyash who could hardly stand. She was limp and lifeless. Her head drooped on her shoulders and her puffed-up body in her tattered dress seemed bereft of strength, as if no blood flowed in it. She didn't cry; her tears were already dried up, so Bronya made up for her by sobbing loudly so that it appeared that she was the mourner and not Mrs Fabyash. No matter how hard Bronya tried to control herself and hold back her tears, she could not. In the end Ida bade her let go of Mrs Fabyash and took her arm herself. Nathan tried to comfort Bronya but did not succeed.

Although she came to the funeral dressed up in her bits and pieces, with even a ribbon round her hair, and in a black dress suitable for the occasion, Bronya soon broke down. All trace of her finery disappeared. Her tears washed the mascara from her eyes and the powder from her cheeks. They ran in little sticky, black streams, streaking her face. On her still youthful face appeared all the wrinkles which she had so cleverly concealed. No sign of her beauty remained.

When the sailors appeared at the other end of the ship, carrying the two bodies that had been enclosed in coffins, hastily made because of the epidemic— one bigger than the other—Mrs Fabyash startled everyone with a shrill scream and then became quiet again. The ship stopped. The sailors carried up the bodies quickly and the captain saluted, standing stiffly to attention. It was so quiet that the heavy tread of the sailors on the deck could be clearly heard. And now the wind blew more strongly and fiercely.

Two gentle splashes were heard. The sea swallowed the two bodies, then rose and subsided as if demanding more. It curled back quickly and broke into tiny, silvery splinters.

'God gives, God takes away. Praise be to God Who is a Just Judge.' It was the voice of Reb Lazar, the grocer.

A wild gust of wind blew in amongst the group and disturbed the doctor's long hair, blowing it in all directions. The sun, big and round, was fastened in the sky like a radiant golden window and shone on Reb Lazar's coat that was the green-red colour of rusty, old iron and on the new rent of mourning on his lapel. Reb Lazar stood quietly and with closed eyes recited the Kaddish, the prayer for the dead. Loudly and distinctly he uttered each word:

'Lord God, hear my voice! At the moment I do not murmur against Thy decree...May his great name be praised for ever and for eternity of eternities.'

Rockman nudged Fabyash, blinking encourage-
ment from his pale, delicate face.

'Say Kaddish, Fabyash,' he urged him, 'say it,
Fabyash.'

Fabyash listened to him and then quickly gabbled
something as if talking to himself. He mumbled the
prayer and when he had finished Reb Lazar could
still be heard chanting the words:

'At this moment I know only one resolve. As my
parent has lived for Thee, so shall my life be dedi-
cated to the glory of Thy name.'

'Disappeared into the water!' someone said. 'At
least when the earth has them one can visit the grave
occasionally.'

The crowd broke up but Mrs Fabyash would not
move from her place. She didn't want to go, saying
that there was plenty of time. What was the hurry?
Hadn't she time to wait?

Fabyash was called to persuade her to go. He
mechanically mumbled a few words to her and
quickly left her. Then suddenly Mrs Fabyash escaped
from Mrs Hudess's and Ida's hands and her swollen
body fell to the ground like a burst sack. They lifted
her and attempted to put her back on her feet but her
legs no longer served her.

Reb Lazar sat down to mourn on an upturned,

low box and removed his shoes. His face was drawn and anguished and he constantly saw his wife before his eyes. She had shared with him all the burdens of their lives. She had been a great housekeeper and she had performed her labours without any fuss. She worked quickly but silently and no one noticed it until everything was finished. Then they marvelled at how well everything was done. And just as quickly as she did everything else, she brought the Sabbath into the house as with a glance. Then, bathed and dressed in honour of the Sabbath, she would come into the shop and send Lazar upstairs. He hadn't eaten since the morning so that he would enjoy more the forthcoming Sabbath meal.

'Go, go, Lazar,' she would urge him. 'Go upstairs to the house. I have already sugared a glass of tea for you. It's on the table. I'll stay here...Go, Lazar.'

When he came up to the house the odours of Sabbath foods were wafted from every corner. The fish was cooling in the clay bowl at the window. The brown, well-baked, twisted loaves were lying on the table and the smell of chicken soup rose from the pot. Not any worse, thanks to God, than in the richest house where there are many maids.

And later, when he came back from prayers, bringing with him a poor man as it is commanded, his wife wouldn't know where to seat him or what to give him, anxious that she might not be doing enough for him.

Once, when a ragged beggar sat at the Sabbath table with them, and the children hadn't been able to take their eyes off his rags and the bare toes that peeped from his shoes, she had been greatly perturbed. A silent and hidden war had taken place between the children and the beggar. The poor man had hidden his shoes under the table in shame, but the children had searched for them and followed them with their gaze. They couldn't take their eyes from the wet muddy stains left by the shoes and finally they could control themselves no longer and burst into speech.

'Look, Mummy,' they gave the poor man away, 'look over there, Mummy!'

But his wife had pretended that she hadn't seen or heard anything but in the end she shouted angrily at the children. She made signs to Lazar, complaining that he did nothing.

'Stop it! Why don't you sit up properly at the table?' she said. 'You're not on your own! Have you lost your manners?'

She had called the children into the kitchen and lectured them for a long time. And when they returned to the table, they no longer stared at the beggar. Although they were still fascinated by his tattered clothes and above all, his worn-out shoes, they controlled themselves and only occasionally gazed fearfully in his direction.

After the meal, as the beggar was about to leave, his wife had stopped him at the door and spoken so that no one could hear:

'Soon, after the Sabbath, you must come back. Don't take it for granted—but, God willing—don't forget.'

And on Saturday night when Lazar was getting ready to go to the Chapel for the meal in honour of the departure of the Sabbath, he had noticed that his wife was searching among his clothes. She had chosen a pair of trousers, a pair of shoes and an old overcoat and made a pack of it. Reb Lazar understood for whom the parcel was intended.

Over Reb Lazar's face there spread a sorrow that gathered in the two deep folds beside his thin, straight nose and in the close web of creases around his open, light-brown eyes. He sat on the low, over-turned box, trying to reckon up the virtues of his wife, may God rest her soul, speaking her praises as is the custom; but he didn't have anyone to listen to him. Suddenly he rose, pushed the box away, and from his face the sadness slowly disappeared. For the Sabbath had arrived.

Reb Lazar pulled on his shoes. He took off his everyday coat, that was torn, and put on in honour of the Sabbath the best that he owned. It was another old coat of the same green-red colour of rusted iron. And so he prepared for the Sabbath. To call together a minyan, ten male Jews over the age of thirteen, was now out of the question. He looked up at the sky. It was sunset. The sun, blood-red, had burst and covered a part of the sky. Like a flooded river, the setting sun poured over the sea, mingled with it and became one with it. Reb Lazar received the Sabbath as he had at the end of every other week, as though he had not just buried his wife. He forgot all his troubles and shed all his daily cares. Quietly he recited the prayers that read:

'Come my beloved, to meet the bride. Let us welcome the presence of the Sabbath. Come my beloved.'

'Come then, in peace, thou crown of thy husband.' He turned to the east and bowed forward three times, welcoming the Sabbath which is likened to a bride.

Then he prepared for the feast of the Sabbath. He took a bit of hard, dry barley and some cold soup that had stood since the morning when he had prepared it and put it aside for the Friday evening meal. Loudly and tunefully he intoned:

'Shalom Aleichem, Peace be unto you, Ye Ministering Angels!'

With joy he received the Sabbath angels, with hardly a tremor in his voice. But when it came to the prayer, 'Who can find a virtuous woman? Her value is far above gems', his voice wavered and he lost himself. His beard was silvered with the tears that coursed down his face. But soon he was himself again. While he ate he sang loudly the Sabbath songs, clapping his hands together.

CHAPTER IX

The raging water rose in an enormous swell and flattened out level with the ship's decks. Then it receded like a mighty, crooked wall, demanding ever more victims.

And the sea received its victims, sucking them quickly down, covering them with foaming angry waters. But still unsatisfied and wailing from the depths, as from some strange underwater world, it shrieked for more. It seemed that the mighty sea was only concerned with the ship that so pitifully rocked and swayed on its lap, that it wanted only to draw this ship into its great abyss.

Soon after Fabyash's little girl, his son departed from this world. The tall, strong boy, who had been

Fabyash's neighbour could not withstand the disease and he went out like a candle. And the Greek lost his wife, whom he was taking back to Australia, and once again he was left quite alone. He had travelled so far to bring a wife from his birth place but he was going back alone to wash his dishes in his little cafe. He still listened to the radio that brought news of his invaded country and his bony fists were more tightly clenched than ever.

Little by little they grew accustomed to hearing the news of more deaths and they no longer went to watch the dead being lowered into the water in sacks weighted with stones. They were afraid of the sight and they avoided it as far as they could. The dead were cast into the sea at night so that no one would see, quietly and without any fuss.

They were heartily tired of each other's company and could hardly bear to look at each other or to hear the same old talk over and over again, nevertheless each morning they carefully glanced around to see that everybody was still there, that the epidemic had not carried one more off overnight. Every morning, friends looked at each other with shining eyes, unable to conceal their relief. Everyone was terrified. If any person noticed the slightest thing—a dizziness, an insignificant blotch on the skin, a tiredness in the legs—he magnified it and was certain that all was over, that at any moment he would fall victim. He would immediately go away from the others so as not to attract attention and wait until he felt better.

When a few days passed without anybody being missed, they secretly believed that, with God's help, the worst was over, but they dared not speak of it openly for fear of tempting the evil eye.

Meanwhile they were assailed by an intense heat that seemed to have fallen from the sky. It came unnoticed, like a plague, and everybody was alarmed.

'Another trouble on our heads. As if we haven't had enough!' they sighed.

'Such terrible heat! Fire is falling from the sky. It has never been so hot!'

In the cabins it was no longer bearable. It was impossible to breathe and sleep was out of the question. The older people tried to remain in the cabins and sleep, but in the middle of the night they crawled out on to the deck with pillows in their hands, searching amongst the old barrels and boxes for a place to rest their heads.

The heat continued for days on end and it was difficult to distinguish between day and night. A grey-white haze enveloped everything and blotted out all shapes and contours. Low, heavy clouds lay

over the ship and in their hot, steaming breath sky
and sea were fused into one dirty, colourless mass.
Sometimes a tongue of light pierced the haze—that
was the only sign of the sun. The whole world lay
breathless and limp and panted for a drink. Everyone expected that rain would fall at any moment and
that they would refresh themselves by drinking cool
water that would pour from the skies. But no rain
came. It seemed that all around the twilight emptiness was an enormous heated oven that spread an
insidious and burning heat. No rain came and the
tiny ration of water that was distributed daily barely
served to moisten their dry, cracked lips.

More than all the rest Marcus Feldbaum and
Mrs Fabyash suffered from thirst. They sat on the
deck, tied together by Fate. When it became hot Mrs
Fabyash was brought up from the cabin and now
she sat like unleavened bread on the deck. She never
moved from her spot and she seemed to melt with
the heat and spread sideways. Marcus Feldbaum had
suffered terribly from hunger, his empty stomach
shrinking and becoming sour and bilious even
when he no longer suffered from seasickness. And
now thirst persecuted him in the same way. He had
forgotten about his hunger and his big eyes, colourless like the sea around him, searched for something

to drink. He even tried to drink the salt water from the tap to quench the fire that burnt within him. He sprang at the tap passionately and was intercepted just in time. With all the strength of his enormous body he continued to throw himself at the tap, shouting loudly and angrily, and it took him a long time to understand what was being said to him.

Everybody went about half naked, shedding one article of clothing after another. The women lost their modesty and shuffled about listlessly in their ragged petticoats from which their naked flesh peeped, just as though there was nothing extraordinary about it. Through their untidy, open blouses could be seen their thin breasts that hung tiredly like empty balloons. The men did not wear shirts, but just pulled on their trousers. Some lounged around in their underpants without the strength to move. They were too exhausted even to look for a corner in which to shelter from the inferno. Everywhere it was the same; everything was scorched by the heat—the old boxes, the barrels that fell out of their hoops, the deck boards, the ropes, the torn tarpaulins. No one could touch the rails and ladders for they glistened with heat and big oily drops stood out on their iron skin.

Although the deck was large enough for everyone to find room to stretch their weary bodies, they all crowded together into one corner and quarrelled over the best place to sleep. They were bad tempered and strained almost to breaking point. They nestled close together, but they could not stand each other, quarrels broke out over trifles and each one insulted the other. It was as though they searched for reasons to quarrel. Sweat poured from half naked bodies and tired snores came from the group as if someone was suffocating.

Many couldn't sleep at all. They wandered around from one place to another, always hoping that some other place would be better and that there they would find sleep.

Nathan and Ida could not close their eyes. They stumbled over the sleeping people in search of a resting place. Nathan trod on someone and immediately a sleepy, angry voice was heard: 'Where are you going? Why don't you be careful? Aren't you used to the dark yet! If you can't see, carry your eyes in your hands. Don't walk on people.'

Nathan quickly withdrew and pulled Ida along with him, both anxious to get away from the place. But the sleepy voice followed them. Nathan fled from the voice, stumbling amongst the lifeboats that gazed towards Heaven with open, black mouths. From the sea rose a vapour as from a boiling cauldron, covering everything like a curtain.

While Ida and Nathan were stumbling around the deck they met others who were unable to sleep. Rockman was wandering about in an unbuttoned shirt and he questioned Nathan closely on the whereabouts of the ship. It must be close to great deserts for where else could such heat spring from? Nathan was an intelligent young man, so he ought to know something about it. Rockman, himself, was not an illiterate and according to his reckoning they should be in the Red Sea. When Nathan told him that he imagined they were near the equator in the Indian Ocean, he had to explain carefully just where that was. And no matter how often he explained, Rockman still wasn't sure and kept asking just whereabouts that was.

On this hot night Rockman was very depressed. All his pride and dignity had left him. He took the captain's part and said that no one could really blame him. The seas were not certain. The Germans had a hand in everything and spread their nets over all seas and ports. The captain was in the soup himself, afraid to go near any port and having to hide at sea. Even when he did put in somewhere he was ordered to go as soon as it was discovered whom he had on board. Now he was afraid to even try, God pity him! The ship was completely at the mercy of others. What did it have to oppose the Germans with? Perhaps it would be of use to send that young woman—what's her name, Bronya?—to the captain. Perhaps she might be able to drag out of him exactly where in the world they were. Who could work out his thoughts and movements? We keep on turning round and round on one spot like a merry-go-round and we never get anywhere. It's a story without an end. And if, with God's help, we do get to Australia, who knows if we'll be allowed to land there? Perhaps our papers are not in order? They don't want to see this little handful of Jews anywhere. Fabyash doesn't always talk through his hat. We've heard of things like this before. What has happened to that young man lately? He's not the same person any more. And he is, after all, an intelligent fellow who knew how to say something. He could sometimes produce a good thought. Of course he is a little wild and thinks a bit much of himself—but that's an old story, for who doesn't think well of himself? A man hangs on and hangs on, but how much can one bear when one is so defenceless? A man is not made of steel.

Rockman spoke the same words that Fabyash had once spoken and held Nathan by the hand, refusing to let him go. But Nathan was tired and had no answer for Rockman. He didn't want to say the same things over and over again, to paddle in the same stream again. Then a quiet and nostalgic voice was heard singing a Polish song. The voice stopped and began to recite with great pathos a poem by a classical Polish writer who poured out his longing for his native land. Nathan recognised the poem. He also recognised the voice of Bronya reciting it. The Polish language was rarely heard on the ship and the well-known words of the poet sounded strange yet so dear and intimate in the middle of the hot sea. But Bronya wasn't allowed to finish the poem; someone interrupted her.

'Poland's finished! You can forget you're Polish,' someone interrupted.

'See how she has begun to sing in the middle of the night! Why, didn't the Pole bring you enough sorrow that you should now yearn for him? You can say the prayer for the dead for him!'

Bronya was silent, not knowing who had spoken. But Noah came to her aid. That Noah, who never had any time for his sister and was always abusing her, took her part.

'Why are you making up the account? What do you mean, that we should pray for a dead Poland?'

'Look who is sticking up for Poland now? Just have a look at Poland's new friend! You said you were in gaol in Poland. Didn't they plague the Jews to death? Didn't they torture them?'

'That's something else. Fascism was responsible for that. The Polish poor didn't want pogroms. They never tortured the Jews.'

'If you're talking so nicely, tell me, why did your friends thrust a knife into Poland's back? Why did they attack the poor worker and peasant from the rear?'

'No one thrust a knife into Poland's back, I can tell you. But the Ruthenian and White Russian people have thrown off their yoke now and the Jews that were saved from German hands apparently don't matter to you. You've just left them out of account.'

'Look now he chants as if from a prayer-book, the Galician! I can see that you know the book off by heart. Well, why did you run away and leave others to stroke the walls of the Russian paradise? A Galician has sense! A Galician philosopher always has his head screwed on the right way. You adore the bride from afar.'

Anything could be said to Noah, but he could not be taunted with the lie that he left when the Red Army was entering his town. That was the worst that could be flung at him—his sorest point. He became very angry. He had always been hot-tempered and acted in the heat of the moment. He was never at a loss for an answer and he never forgave an injustice. Now everything boiled over and his body quivered. Back home in Lvov he had more than once argued with the neighbours who came to his parents' house and would not agree with his ideas. Although they were poor, without a piece of bread in the house, they had refused to accept the truth that he saw so clearly he could touch it. He had found this difficult to understand and in his excitement he had insulted and quarrelled with his neighbours. And now he was ready to answer the one who had so deeply wounded him. But suddenly voices came from every side.

'Let us sleep! Let us close our eyes. Find some other place to quarrel. Get away from here.'

When he heard the shouts growing louder and more heated, Noah's words stuck in his throat and he made no answer.

Nathan listened to the argument. The voice that abused Noah was familiar to him, but no matter how hard he tried he could not make out whose it was. He was thinking of Poland now conquered and overrun. He remembered the boarding houses that he had lived in in Warsaw. The shrill cries of the vendors and tradesmen, who had continually filled the courtyards with their noise, rang in his ears. How the owners of those boarding houses had plagued him! They had talked him to death, pursued him for rent and he had often had to hide from them to fool them, so that his life was hardly worth living. He had dreamed of journeying abroad and he had studied with determination to get somewhere, to extricate himself from the bog. He sat far into the night by the smoky kerosene lamp, afraid to keep the gas burning late for fear of the owner and the strange fellows who slept in the same room with him. He stared long at the patched and rusty camp stretcher and at the untidy, crumpled bedclothes that his mother had washed, mended and packed into a sack along with a jar of jam. That had been just before he left home and he remembered his mother's big, honest masculine hands. He sat over his books late into the night, straining his eyes and wetting his burning forehead with cold water but never straightening his bowed shoulders.

For all his diligent studying the years had passed quickly and brought no results. He had bitten his nails in determination, as was his habit while studying, but he had seen no future before him.

Many obstacles had been placed in his way. He wasn't allowed to study what he wanted to. He threw himself from one thing to another and his head was always full of plans that all came to nothing. He had watched his Polish friends get everywhere, do whatever they desired, and he was pushed out of everything. He had had to watch, and swallow his frustration.

Although Nathan had been weary of everything, now he harboured no resentment for all that had passed. On the contrary he felt nostalgic for the boarding houses with the ill-tempered landladies, the dilapidated houses on Mille Street, where he had lived, for the shrill cries of the second-hand vendors and even for the teachers who had made his road so difficult. He remembered his poor father with his shrunken beard and dried-up lips, his torn coat with a few pins always peeping out from the lapel. And all the time he kept anxiously pushing back his tradesman's cap. Nathan could clearly see his father and then before his eyes appeared the township and the respectable citizens who did him the honour of shaking his hand, the girls who strolled up and down the marketplace, the Jews with the prayer shawls on their shoulders who came away from their prayers with slow thoughtful steps.

He remembered a wedding that had taken place at night in the township, near the synagogue in the middle of the marketplace. He saw again a grandmother with a shawl over her head and a loaf of bread in her hand dance towards the bride and bridegroom. He saw the fireworks that spread greenish stars in the night and the melting tallow of guttering candles. He saw outstretched children's hands and heard the players grow now jolly, now sad. Polish people stood around with the Jews of the township and watched everything, shaking hands with the relatives and wishing them 'Mazel Tov'.

Nathan remembered staying with his grandfather in a village when he was very small. He was spending his school vacation at his grandfather's where there was plenty of good food. He was to put flesh over his bones while he was in the village. His grandfather had taken him every Saturday to pray in a synagogue with hanging brass lamps and a small, sombre altar. He had read from the big, leather, gold-embossed prayer book with his grandfather. It was the only one in the district and Nathan had loved the book so much that he didn't skip one word of the prayers.

His grandfather had always promised to leave the prayer book to him. And when his grandfather died he took it for himself after the funeral, when the low, whitewashed room was full of village Jews and peasants who would have laid down their lives for the old man, who affectionately called him 'Berek'. Nathan quietly pushed a stool up to the shelf where the prayer book lay and furtively hid it under his coat. Then he walked off home with his inheritance.

The village road smelt of freshly cut hay. The sun streamed down on the leaves of the trees, curled itself round their branches and trembled in the golden dust that rose behind every passing wagon. A solitary frog in a nearby pool, unable to wait for the evening, woke up and croaked sleepily. And a stork with slow strides walked the peaceful fields, looking around like a proprietor. In the wayside shrine where candles burnt continually, little girls with flaxen hair covered the statue of the Virgin with bouquets of flowers that they gathered in the fields. Village Jews plodded home from the market, perspiring and covered in dust. Peasant youths in coarse linen shirts and girls in wide, red-checked, billowing skirts worked in the fields. As Nathan passed them he uttered the words that his grandfather had taught him to use when he met a person working on the land: 'Praised be God'.

As it became dark the fields began to talk in hidden voices and Nathan still had a long way to go. His heart began to thump as he remembered his dead grandfather and his strides became longer.

The prayer book scorched his hands and caused him great anxiety. A peasant from his grandfather's village overtook him and, glancing respectfully at his college cap, asked him if he was Berek's grandson and son of Mr Rieff, the hatmaker in the town. Then he helped him into the wagon and took him home.

All the rest of his holidays he spent in the town. He and his Jewish and Christian friends, who were also on holiday, paraded in their school uniforms.

But later, when he went home on holiday, it became lonely and gloomy. After he left secondary school and could not get into the courses he wanted, his Christian friends who had finished their studies and were now in good positions, had nothing more to do with him. In the town Jews were being beaten. A frail Jew, Sisha Sim Michaelis, was so badly beaten that he nearly died. Then his Christian friends felt embarrassed before Nathan and avoided meeting his eyes. But later they pretended not to know him and even began to take part in slanders against the Jews.

Nathan looked around and noticed that Ida was no longer at his side. The heat had not lessened; it was as humid and sticky as before. The sky was low and heavy over the sea and bulged with heavy clouds. For a moment the moon shone through, glittering like a lance, and then it was quickly hidden again. The sea stirred lazily, barely disturbing the sleepy, puffy waves and it seemed that the ship stood still.

Nathan searched for Ida and found her standing alone, far away from anyone. She reproached him for having allowed her to go away. He must be thoroughly tired of her if he didn't notice whether she was near him or not.

Ida was very angry but she felt helpless and lost. She complained that Nathan didn't pay any attention to her. He must have had enough of her. She felt neglected. Whom did she have but Nathan? And when he no longer looked at her it was very hard for her.

As soon as she uttered these words she regretted them and wanted to withdraw them. She shouldn't have said that. She shouldn't have shown Nathan so openly what was going on within her. But it was too late. She felt so sad and dejected now. She had never revealed herself to Nathan before. She had always carefully measured her words and never given him a clue. No matter how much she had wanted to tell him what was in her heart, to nestle her head against him and take hold of his hands to stroke her hot face, she had never in any circumstances allowed herself that.

Her husband, Hershl, who had remained somewhere at home and whom she had hated from the
depths of her heart because he stood between her
and Nathan, would not allow her to do that. He tied
her hands. She knew that it would be an injustice
to Hershl, to whom she should now do no evil, and
above all an injustice to her child, her Sarah, whom
she had borne to him. And apart from all that, she
didn't want to reveal her feelings for Nathan.

Although she knew that it wasn't really so, nevertheless she always imagined that Nathan thought of
himself as superior to Hershl, looking down upon
him, and was just waiting for her to forget herself.
And for this reason she would never favour him
with a pleasant word, but always drove him away,
although she knew she was hurting him. The deeply-
buried sinful thought that both Nathan and she were
using the great tragedy that had befallen their nearest
never left her for one moment, and always gnawed
at her and tortured her. Now that their hands were
freed they could be together. It almost seemed as if
they had waited for just that.

It was almost too much for her. She had wanted
not to meet Nathan again—never to be seen with
him again. People had already talked enough and
were keeping a sharp eye on them. But no sooner

had Nathan left her for a time without seeing her than she began to long for him again. She longed for him even though she knew he was still on the ship with her. She was overjoyed every time she caught a glimpse of him, even from a distance. She was delighted to see the familiar, beloved face that she knew so well, for it had disappeared completely from her mind when she didn't see him. When Nathan wasn't with her she couldn't remember what he looked like and she became afraid. She had to dig deeply into her memory to recall his soft grey eyes, his unshaven, hollow cheeks, longish nose, slightly stooped shoulders and his narrow figure.

Then she would go to look for him, peering into every corner, afraid that something might have happened to him, but all the time pretending that she wasn't looking for him. Later, when she had him near her, she didn't know why she had been so excited and upset. The face that she had so longed for and not been able to recall now appeared ordinary—a face like that of any other young man. When Nathan saw the state she was in, he asked her why she was so restless and upset. She found excuses from everywhere so that she would not reveal herself.

But now she had disclosed her feelings and Nathan well remembered the words she had used.

He had only heard such words from her before on one occasion. A few words had escaped her on that beautiful, calm morning when he had told her about his plans as they stood together near the deck rails. He was overcome with joy that she had now forgotten herself and revealed her feelings for him. He felt proud and grew taller in his own eyes. The man in him that had been suppressed now came to life.

That morning Ida hadn't wanted to talk to him and turned her head away. She was exhausted with the heat although she would not admit it. From a distance he had observed that she went about as the other women did, with an open blouse and a loose skirt, undone, so that it looked as though it would fall down at any moment. Without any modesty she had pulled her skirt up well above her knees which were the golden colour of honey, but Nathan noticed that her skin above her knees was gleaming white. It was the first time he had seen her body so revealed and he had not guessed that her skin would be so transparently white. That very paleness had confused him so that he turned his head away, not to look in her direction. But his eyes were drawn to her again and he saw her brown, chestnut hair so carelessly shorn at the time of the disinfection making her look like a naughty, stubborn boy. Nathan noticed that as her hair had grown a little she had trimmed and styled it so that it curled lightly over her thin, girlish neck and on her forehead. Her carelessly cut hair now added to her charm and he was overcome with sympathy for her.

Nathan had often wondered about her, trying to discover in what way she was different from other women and what it was he saw in her. When she was scantily clad he clearly saw her shoulders and bare arms. She lifted her arms and ran her fingers through her short hair, smoothing it back from her brow and her neck so that it would be cooler for her. Her gestures were abrupt and severe, yet at the same time girlish. Her neck was uncovered, long and slim and proudly erect like a white tower.

Ida was then suffering from the heat and Nathan wished he could make it easier for her by giving her some hope. But as he came closer to her she averted her head and quickly pulled down her dress and her fingers dexterously buttoned up her blouse, right up to the neck as if to spite herself, even though it was so hot.

Now Nathan embraced Ida, at the same time making excuses for himself. But she didn't even listen properly to him; every word he uttered was wasted and she would not allow him to defend himself. All his talk seemed unnecessary to her and the more tenderness he revealed, the cooler she became and the more angry. His gentleness was unwanted and she couldn't understand why he was so close to her, nor why, a moment before, she had been so excited and so anxious for a good word from him. Her child and her husband came to her mind and she spoke their names aloud and wept softly; Nathan's arm that had encircled her so closely and pressed her so strongly to him now only offended her.

But Nathan would not release her and stroked her short curls that fell over her neck. Her hot tears fell on his fingers. And just as at home when her father had hit her and Nathan had torn her out of his hands and soothed her, so now her tears aroused him. One hand caressed her trembling, girlish shoulders and the tears that he allowed to run over the other filled him with delight and a desire to press her to him until she cried out in pain.

She pushed him away but he held her firmly, refusing to let her go. And then he shouted at her so that she was frightened of him. In the darkness he felt her full lips a little chapped and split. He had always had a great desire to kiss them and now he searched with his lips for the dent that divided her upper lip and kissed her so hard that her teeth collided with his.

'Why are you so cruel? Why are you so bitter?' he murmured straight into her hot, dry mouth.

She made no answer. Nathan's hand that so freely and impudently roamed over her loose dress and every fold of her body, which shone white in the darkness, no longer offended her. Their hot breaths mingled and her lips, twisted with pain and desire, freed themselves to cry out once more, soberly and warningly:

'Nathan!'

But soon there was no more warning in her voice. She repeated the one word, 'Nathan,' but now she spoke it with affection and with all the longing that for many years she had carried.

Then she said nothing more and thought no more. There was no one else in the world but herself and Nathan. Later she even forgot that.

CHAPTER X

After that sweltering night Nathan and Ida avoided meeting each other. She couldn't look him straight in the face and harboured a great resentment towards him. She felt guilty and all her guilt she placed on Nathan. He should not have behaved as he had; he ought not to have forgotten himself. She rarely left the cabin and went to the dining room late, when Nathan would no longer be there. Although often enough she wanted to go to the dining room on time so that she could meet him unexpectedly, and even left the cabin punctually with this resolve, yet as soon as she was on her way her steps began to falter and she followed side passages so that in the end she was late. But when she entered the room and

Nathan was not there her heart sank and she felt a great longing for him, reproaching herself for not coming on time.

Nathan also felt guilty and avoided Ida. He felt in his mind the warmth of his son's hand that back home had led him to his mother, not letting him look at his Aunt Ida. His heart was constricted with suffering and he felt that Ida was avoiding him. So he too avoided the places where he might meet her, coming late or leaving before she appeared. But he also wanted to see her, and although he pretended that he didn't, he lay in wait for her so that he might unexpectedly run into her. But always at the last moment he wavered and went away with an emptiness in his heart. Although he knew that Ida was not far away, and in his mind's eye he could see her at the deck rails, on the spiral steps that led to the cabins and in every corner where they had ever met, the feeling that he had lost forever something near and dear clung to him.

The heat had waned; it no longer burned so fiercely. The days stretched long, although night fell quickly and without warning. Bronya Feldbaum didn't know what to do with herself during the day and waited impatiently for night, when she could meet the well-groomed steward. On the day after the night when the women had so grievously insulted her, she had wandered around chastened and contrite and it was believed that a great change had overcome her. But soon after midday she forgot all about it. She was the same Bronya of old; not a hair on her head had altered. She decked herself out in her bits and pieces scratched up from here and there and put together with a skill that only women possess. Even pieces of men's clothes went into the making of her finery. And she tied up her short, clipped hair in curl papers so that she resembled a sheep.

Bronya cajoled the eminent Warsaw doctor's tiny wife into playing cards with her during the day. She had long wanted to be friends with the doctor's wife and she was very happy when the other lady agreed to play with her. She thoroughly enjoyed her new social position.

The doctor's wife was a skilful card player. She was the daughter of very rich parents, from amongst the half assimilated wealthy Jews of Warsaw. After her marriage, when she didn't have much to do, she had often invited rich women like herself to a game of cards. There was little else to do in the big, spacious rooms of her Warsaw home. She looked after her only son, and above all, cared for her husband, who was more trouble than the child. He couldn't look after himself and would have gone about neglected, without having anything to eat for days on end, if she hadn't cared for him. More than once he went out in winter without his coat when the frost was heavy, and he had put on his fur coat in the summer.

Her job had been to watch his every step, brush his clothes, give him his meals and even peel him the occasional orange. It had been the same on the boat, where she followed him with a bowl and forced every spoonful of food upon him. And just as at home where her husband had been absorbed in his surgery and had never had any time for her, so on the ship he had no interest in her. He begged her to leave him alone and he wandered busily about, talking to people and gazing into their faces with his kindly, patient, half-senile eyes.

The doctor's anxious wife was ready to play cards with Bronya. Perhaps it would help her to forget her worries about her husband, for whom she had the greatest respect as for a stranger, although it was now many years since their wedding. There was only one obstacle in her way; she didn't want to play for money. She had always been cautious and known the value of a penny—she was no spendthrift. Although she had a little money that she carried on her person for safety, and a few valuable jewels that she had saved, she didn't want to touch them. She guarded them like the eyes of her head, for they were to restore her husband's lost health in the land to which they were travelling.

But Bronya had no intention of playing for money. She merely wanted to while away the time. An idea occurred to her: they would play with bits of paper, and she made some banknotes from an old piece of paper. She wrote in figures the value of each note.

The game began and Bronya won. The pile of paper in front of her kept growing. She became so excited with the game that she saw nothing else and she began to count the paper as if it were real. Every piece of paper that she won she guarded, and in her eyes it assumed the value of real money. And she became quite serious, treating the paper as a debt owed to her by the doctor's wife. She told her that there was no hurry; she was not wanting the money immediately; she would wait.

But the doctor's wife would have none of it. She became alarmed and, closing her short-sighted eyes like a hen, spoke in a quiet, refined voice that couldn't hurt a fly. 'We made an arrangement, Mrs Feldbaum. Don't you remember? You can't have forgotten.'

One word led to another and the women began

to attack each other. It went so far that Bronya demanded that the doctor's wife take out her jewels and pay her debt. She threw accusations at the doctor's wife that there were heretics in her family. She said that it wasn't right for an honest, virtuous Jewish daughter as she was to have any association with her.

They spoke quietly so that no one overheard and Rockman envied the women because they had found something to do.

Reb Zainval Rockman went about on his own.

Nobody wanted to listen yet again to his endless stories of his two sons or to his musings on whether Jews should be faithful to God or man to have some firm foundation beneath their feet. Rockman's one dream was to find someone to play chess with.

'A game of chess would suit me right down to the ground! That's a sensible game.'

He stopped everyone that he met to urge a game upon them.

'It would help us to forget some of our troubles,' he said.

Rockman would even listen to the radio now, although it always brought news of more German victories. It seemed as though the Germans, who were conquering one country after another, were chasing the ship and would soon overtake it. More than once several aeroplanes had appeared over the ship flying in formation. But to whom they belonged no one knew because they flew so high. Everyone became frightened and the ship cowered on the water, shrinking like a clucking hen that has seen an eagle.

Reb Zainval Rockman didn't want to think about anything. He searched for a game of chess and even stopped Reb Lazar, the grocer, to ask him whether he played.

But Reb Lazar had something else to do. The day passed quickly for him. He hardly looked around before the day was over. His prayers occupied several hours and between prayers he recited psalms and chanted audibly from a holy book. He complained to Rockman that even on Saturday the Jews rarely came together to pray as a congregation. He didn't, God forbid, want to interfere with anyone else. It wasn't his affair and he didn't want to preach to anyone else at a time when he himself wasn't free from sin. Who was he, after all, an ordinary mortal of flesh and blood, to preach to anyone? It was not his place to put himself in the position of leader, of one who has received a call. He couldn't place himself above others. But after all, in such bitter times, Jews should hold more firmly to their Jewishness. Why shouldn't they look into the Holy Book occasionally and now and then recite a chapter of Psalms? Man does not live by bread alone. If Jews remembered God more often, perhaps the Almighty would pay more attention to them.

Reb Lazar had enough to fill out his days with. Since his wife, may she rest in peace, departed from this world, he had to look after himself. That was hard for him. He couldn't take any food that was not kosher, even if he knew it meant that he would die of hunger. Previously his wife had looked after his food, now he had to do everything himself. He found it hard to approach the sleepy but well-disposed cook who still couldn't understand why he wouldn't eat with the others and insisted on doing his own cooking. Reb Lazar tried to make him understand, giving him examples and pointing with his hands, but it could not penetrate the cook's head. He laughed at Reb Lazar, and his mouth full of big, white teeth gleamed in his plump, olive-dark face.

The cook was never in a hurry. Since he began to get very friendly with Noah he looked with different eyes on the Jews. The friendship began when the cook talked to Noah and told him that his dream was to visit Russia and to see Communism come to

his home-country, Greece. He concealed a corner of
his kitchen from the captain. There he had written
some slogans in crude and twisted letters. He had
drawn a hammer and sickle and covered it with a
small red flag. He called the corner his 'red corner'
and spent all his free time there, reading a book or
singing songs in a sleepy voice. He had also inscribed
a hammer and sickle with chalk on a few blackened
tins and frying pans.

As soon as the cook became acquainted with
Noah he invited him into the kitchen and his plump,
gentle face beamed as he pointed out his 'corner'.
His excitement was so great that he seized Noah in
his big, bear-like hands and kissed him in front of
all the Jews. His giant-like, well-developed body was
filled with joy. Noah was embarrassed and pulled
away from his arms, but the cook wouldn't let him
go, repeating over and over again the same thing:
'Comrade!'

He slapped Noah on the back and disconcerted
him with the praise that he liberally bestowed upon
him. 'With me all men are equal, as in Russia, Turks,
Jews, Chinese, Greeks. With me all men are broth-
ers. Red blood flows in everyone's veins. Give me
your hand, comrade. Shake for the new world that is
coming soon.'

He clasped Noah's hand and shook it firmly up and down.

Noah stood as if held in a vice and did not know how to answer. Those words of the cook that he understood moved him deeply, and he was pained that he was silent and unable to bring out the words he wanted to say. The other Jews were also moved by the cook's excitement and his friendliness warmed their hearts. Nevertheless they teased Noah for finding for himself such a good comrade with whom he could be good friends and take a bite together.

For Rockman, it was as if the cook had fallen from Heaven. He had searched every corner without finding a chess set when it occurred to him to go to the cook and ask him about it. And the cook dug up a chess set from somewhere. In truth the board and the men were old and broken. The colour had faded so that it was impossible to tell white from black— but still it was better than nothing. Rockman soon found a way to distinguish the pieces. He tied some black thread around the necks of the black pieces. Then he went to look for Nathan and they sat down for a game.

Rockman enjoyed playing. He was very dignified and he continually moved his skullcap about on his head with his delicate white hands. Whenever he was deeply absorbed in a move his cap sat so low on his forehead that it nearly fell off. He needed only a cigarette to help him organise his thoughts. In his agitation he kept on thrusting his fingers into his vest pocket in which lay the empty cigarette case, forgetting that it was a long time since there had been any cigarettes there.

Although he often thought for a long while before making a move, especially when he was cornered, he complained that Nathan was slow. The heat made Rockman puff into his beard and whenever he was in a dangerous position he thought aloud, talked to himself and allowed his hand to stray over the chessboard. He could dawdle and take time to think, but no one else could.

'If I go here with the rook, he'll go there.' He thought aloud in a chant.

'If I go there, he'll go there. I'm already cornered! And how am I to crawl out of this, my friend?'

Rockman had a high opinion of his own game and wanted everyone to see his brilliant moves. But if people stood around and gave him advice he really suffered. He hated advice-givers like poison. Whenever he was advised about a move he would say nothing, but he would slowly rise from his chair and invite the audacious fellow to take his place.

'Be seated.' With affected patience he would point out his chair. 'If you're so clever you may take over the game. Let's see how good you are! Well?'

But it was even worse when he was losing. Then he would quite forget himself. He would grab the king and put it in his pocket and nothing would make him return it.

'I won't give you the king,' he would say excitedly, waving his hands, 'you haven't won the game as far as I'm concerned. The king is in my pocket. I won't give it up!'

Rockman played with everybody and it was a matter of life and death for him that Fabyash should play with him and forget some of his sorrows. But Fabyash did not even hear him when he spoke and did not know what he wanted. He was now so completely withdrawn into himself that he associated with no one. He was convinced that the ship would never arrive anywhere, that all their papers were false, that something was wrong somewhere so that no place would ever allow this little group of Jewish refugees to land anywhere. The captain must have taken a very big bribe for carrying us. He won't admit anything, but God knows where that Jew-hating captain is taking us. Fabyash is certain that he is taking them right into the arms of the Germans.

Why else do we always have to hide far out at sea? Then what is the use of their long journey? It would be better to make an end of everything quietly.

Fabyash can no longer look his wife in the face. She always sits in the same spot and stares into space. He can't stand her staring eyes. They give him no peace; they follow him wherever he goes and accuse him:

'Murderer! It is your fault. You are responsible for everything.' Her eyes seem to scream at him. 'You killed my child. If not for you, everything would still have been all right! Your cowardice, your fear for your own skin, was the cause. Why did you allow the child to go around with the disease? Why didn't you say something? It might have been caught in time and then everything would have been different. You killed my daughter and my son! You madman!'

Fabyash avoided his wife. If only she were not always so silent. If she would have spoken one word to him! Her silence was worse than anything she could have said. Her silence was profoundly eloquent and it pierced him deeply, wounding and torturing him.

Fabyash told no one about all this; he confided in no one. But it weighed heavily upon him. He was no longer afraid of anything; it was all the same to him now. If no one else showed any fear, why should he be an exception? Why should he disgrace himself before others? Nobody would listen to him anyway—no one wanted to understand him. Even his own wife didn't want to understand him and seldom even looked at him.

Everyone pitied him and it was just from pity that they still spoke to him. He felt it deeply for he knew what was going on. For as long as he could remember he had not been well liked and even as a youth the other boys had avoided him. There must be something about him that made people dislike him.

He remembered that he had always gone his own way when he was a boy in Ger. When he grew up he was always quarrelling with his father. His father, Reb Fishel, had been an orchardist with some property and a strict Hassid disciple of the Gerer rabbi. For the rabbi he would have given his life; he would have made any sacrifice. He was ready to attack anyone who so much as uttered a word against the rabbi, to tear him to pieces. But he was far from being a learned Talmudist. In fact he was a long way from being a scholar at all.

Fabyash's father had been a small man, with an untidy beard, but he was full of self-assurance and audacity. He spoke with great familiarity to older men, preaching and shouting at them as if they were little boys. Yet he was extremely pious and was always ready to welcome into his house the poor Hassidim, the followers of the rabbi, who could not afford to go to lodgings and could not find a place in the rabbi's courtyard. These Hassidim often slept on the hay in his barn and sometimes they even lay in the fruit sheds so that every corner was filled.

They would quarrel amongst themselves, arguing over the scriptures, as they wandered, with their prayer-shawl fringes hanging loose, through the high grass of the orchard and amongst the trees whose branches were bent to the earth under the weight of fruit bursting with sweet juice. His father took pride in his own ignorance and would declare loudly that the only thing that mattered was fear of the Lord. He was suspicious of clever scholars and argued that those young men who were bookworms were the first to desert the faith. So he never felt comfortable when the Hassidim were arguing about the scriptures for he didn't understand much of what they were saying.

His son, Fabyash, did know what the arguments were about. He was a good scholar but even then he had moved away from all that. His faith in his father's beliefs had gone long ago. He had even been out walking with a girl, secretly. He had used a powder to remove his soft, sprouting beard, so that his cheeks were always smooth. His father, who was always busy, noticed nothing until one day a Hassid opened his eyes.

'Ha! Fishel, I've heard some nice stories about your Nehemiah.' He spoke to his father, but he held Fabyash firmly so that he couldn't run away.

'Your pride and joy has been seen wandering around with a girl! It seems to me that he's been possessed by the devil. He's deserted his faith! Have a good look at him. His beard is not growing! What's the matter with him, Fishel? And look at his crop of hair. There's not even room for the phylacteries!'

His father approached him and peered at him from close-up and he saw that the Hassid was right. He delivered two fierce blows that resounded loudly.

'Here's for the beard, and here's for the girl!' His father counted the blows. 'I'll tear you up by the roots, you larrikin! You heretic! I'll kill you on the spot ! You rascal! You enemy of Israel! Get out of my house, you Christian! You...'

Fabyash left the house immediately, taking the fiery marks of his father's fingers on his cheeks. He and his father had remained enemies; he had even married without his father's consent. But he had inherited his father's assertiveness. He was always jumping at everybody and he thought he knew everything; there was nothing in the world that was new to him—he had heard everything before. But the self-assurance of his father he didn't have in him. He carried around a constant fear, an unrest that never left him alone, as though someone was always standing behind his back.

He had been certain that he would make a stir in the world as soon as he left his father, who had never permitted him to go into business. But his business hadn't gone well and he had had to remain at a trade. He ran a little workshop where he made jackets and trousers for the peasants. And although he worked day and night he barely made a living. From all the scraps he made something which he took home for his wife and children. He would have had enough to eat and not had to work so hard in his workroom but for the unrest that stirred in him and the fear of the morrow that never left him.

He struggled so hard all these years and finally worked himself up to something. But it was his fate to lose, at one blow, everything that he had scratched together with his fingernails through all these hard years. When the world was on fire around him and every minute was precious because all the time life was in grave peril, he piled in an open wagon all the goods that he had gathered together at such cost to his health and strength. He didn't want to give them up and he wasn't concerned for his life, for without his possessions the world no longer had any meaning for him. He worked to his last ounce of strength, bathed in sweat, his shirt wringing wet. He kept running in and out of the house, piling more and more domestic utensils onto his back until his small body was bent to the earth. He even wanted to take the furniture with him and by himself he carried out the big, heavy table, but he was hardly able to do anything with it, like an ant that carries too heavy a splinter. People laughed at him and treated him as a fool. The driver hurried him on, shouted at him and cursed him, threatening that he would leave him and all his goods behind. But Fabyash was deaf to the laughter and the shouts. His wife stood as if on hot coals and blocked the door of the house.

'Madman!' she exploded, not knowing what to do with him. 'Where are you taking all these things? You are mad! Save your life first. What are you doing? What will you do with all these things? You are murdering your children! Oh people, I can't do anything with him! Our lives are in danger.

Every minute you waste is a great sin!'

But he didn't listen to her. He didn't want to hear what she said and couldn't make out what she wanted of him. His beady eyes stared at her and sped distraughtly from side to side like frightened mice.

When at last he was ready to leave, it was too late. The Germans caught up with them on the way and they turned the loaded wagon over with the children on top. They stuck the naked shiny bayonets into his possessions, almost stabbing the children, and reduced everything to a mountain of rubble. He fell full length on the remains with both hands outstretched as though he wanted to die with all his goods. His wife just managed to pull him away, but it was the cries of his children who wept over him as over a corpse that tore him from the earth. For the rest of the journey his wife gave him no peace, continually reproaching him. She would remain silent for a little while only to begin scolding more strongly and more insistently.

'It's a good job that it happened to you!' She derived some pleasure from his misery and resumed her scolding like a toothache that stops for a moment only to begin afresh to nag more sharply and stubbornly than before.

'You've got a mad mind! What people say about

you is only too true. I certainly fell in properly with you!'

His wife's justified reproaches and the fear in his children's eyes when the gleaming naked bayonets passed so close to them, always pursued him, eating at him like a worm. Nor could his conscience ever escape from his daughter's feverish face when she told him that she wasn't well and he had not wanted to believe her and had shouted angrily at her, making her wander about with the illness. He could always see his daughter's eyes, tired and sick with the high fever that had possessed her. They stare at him from the sea where the child's body has rested for some time. He can still hear clearly the gentle splash of his daughter being lowered into the water. What had the child ever had in her life? No happiness had she enjoyed with him and now she was cut off from life. When he looks at the sea he hears that sound, no matter how quiet the water is.

But he is no longer afraid of the sea as he was at the beginning of the journey. Then, when everyone was learning how to put on the lifebelts he hid as far away from them as he could. Now it doesn't worry him any more; it is a game for him just as for the children. He looks indifferently at the lifeboat and no longer hides so that he has to be called or searched for.

He stares at the sea that lies peacefully and complacently with only a slight swell, but has all the colours of the rainbow. Here the sea is green, here blue, here shimmering in the sun like mother-of-pearl. He forgets entirely that it is the sea he watches, forgets entirely where he is. He is on the banks of the Vistula at Ger, walking out with his wife. She is not his wife but his fiancée. His wife's puffy, doughy figure becomes smaller and smaller. She is so thin that he can encircle her waist with his hands, just as he could do when she was his fiancée. His wife is again the slender young girl with long plaits twined round her head. The Vistula is lit by the sun and lies smooth and flat, gleaming like an iron roof amongst the thick green of gardens and fields. The orchards near the Vistula are fragrant and breathe forth a rich sweet-sour perfume. He is a little boy running with a group of school fellows to bathe in the river on a hot July day. Although it is quite a distance away the schoolboys are lured to bathe in the Vistula and it seems to them that they are doing something heroic. Flushed and serious, they run quickly and furtively so that no one should see them, especially their fathers who could punish them. He throws himself into the water which splashes in little glassy balls around his boyish body. It is pleasantly cool and slaps him delightfully as if with innumerable silver canes. He floats and sees above him the clean, blue sky, the water refreshes and gives him new life; it is so pleasant...like the sea around him. He is amongst the lifeboats, just where there are no rails. And just one step and the water will enfold his body and splash round him in a silvery dust just like the Vistula. He will again become a child and everything will be easy again, pleasantly easy...

Fabyash suddenly awoke and he was overcome by fear. He stood on the edge of the deck and just one false step and he would fall into the sea. He was full of self-pity. His own emaciated, withered skin, at which he had never cast a glance became dear to him. His heart constricted.

His head began to swim and a terrible fear gripped him so that he gave a cry. But no one heard his cry; all around was empty and not a person was to be seen. Only the sea rolled innocently and peacefully. He pulled himself away because he felt that some power was drawing him towards the water. He ran quickly to where there were people, mixing with them and nestling closer to them. His small eyes blinked fearfully and the brush-like stubble that he had grown stood out strange and prickly with a rusty-red colour in the middle. Until now, this strange, hard growth had not been noticeable but at this moment it was so obvious that it caught every eye. People moved away from him, and above all from his sprouting beard that seemed so different, as though it had grown overnight.

Fabyash wandered amongst the people and noticed Reb Lazar reading out of a sacred book. He sat down next to him. Reb Lazar didn't interrupt his reading, although he was conscious that Fabyash had sat down by him. He just moved a little to make more room, dumbly showed him where he was up to on the page, and went on murmuring as he had before, inviting Fabyash to read with him.

Fabyash longed to immerse himself in the sacred book but he couldn't absorb anything; nothing would enter his head. He moved quietly away from Reb Lazar. His place remained vacant for Reb Lazar did not move back, as if he was waiting for Fabyash to change his mind and return. Fabyash ran down to his wife in the cabin and for the first time since the misfortune had befallen her legs asked her if she would like to go up to the deck where it was not so close as down below. He would call someone and they would carry her up. But his wife didn't answer him, not even turning her head.

All alone Fabyash went back up the dark,

winding stairs. His mind was in a fog, and only single thoughts tore through. Why didn't people feel what was going on in him? Why didn't someone try to come nearer to him? Nobody wanted to save him, to prevent him from doing what, at any moment, he was going to do. It tormented him, it hurt him. He could see that everything was lost. He had lost himself and he couldn't find his way back. Nobody came to his aid. Nobody could see how bad things were with him. Why did everyone still repulse him? To the last moment people remained harsh to him.

His mind was still in a fog; he couldn't free himself from it. He didn't see where he was going, nor did he feel what he was doing. He felt a chill in his bones and, looking around, he saw that he was standing near the lifeboats again, just where there were no rails. Some power had drawn him to that spot. Just one more step and he would feel sun-drenched water around his body, just as when he was a lad and bathed in the Vistula. It would become easy again, so easy; a heavy weight would be lifted from him.

CHAPTER XI

All night Mrs Fabyash tossed and turned on the bunk, unable to close an eye. Sleep had deserted her. She was constantly listening to the merest sound, to every creak that came from the steps, waiting for her husband to come in. She could feel in the dark the empty place where her husband slept. A heavy, sour odour from the sleeping bodies pervaded the air so that it was difficult to breathe. From a corner came snoring and whistling and from a far-off cabin floated the sad, reflective songs of sailors.

Mrs Fabyash listened in the darkness, turning from side to side. She heard the movements of the ship, all its limbs throbbing, and the grunting, clanging engines breathed like human beings as the ship ponderously and bluntly cleaved the waves. Apprehension never left Mrs Fabyash and the empty space beside her made her more afraid. She wanted to look for her husband and sat up on her bunk. She even tried to put her feet to the floor, looking around in every corner as if she was waiting for help from somewhere. But her feet were as stiff as wood and a sharp pain shot through her and gripped her whole body, draining her last ounce of strength. She fell back on the bunk in a cold sweat. Involuntarily she began to call to the people around her. But everyone was sunk in such a deep sleep that no one heard her calls. Someone woke for a moment, asked her something, said something disjointed and then immediately fell asleep again.

Mrs Fabyash began to delude herself that everything was just a horrible dream, that her husband was sleeping in his place and that nothing had happened. In a weak voice she called to her husband, but no one answered her. She waited for daylight, persuading herself that she would find him in his bunk as usual. And when morning crept into the cabin slowly and sleepily, she was afraid to turn to her husband's empty bunk, for she was now quite certain that no one was lying there. She gave a shriek and awakened everyone. Nobody knew what was the matter and she said nothing, but dumbly pointed to her husband's empty bunk. Then she pointed to the door which was always left open so that there would be no panic in the event of the ship meeting with an accident that would necessitate the passengers hastening up on deck. The open door was like an evil omen that cast over everybody fear and anxiety as if a strange, angry sentry was on guard there. More than anybody else Fabyash had been afraid of the open door and had always wanted to close it. More than one quarrel had occurred with him over that door.

Everybody was still drowsy and could not understand why Mrs Fabyash was pointing to the door and her husband's empty bunk. But suddenly it became clear and sleep disappeared. In its place came clearheadedness and understanding, as if every separate person had been douched with a bucket of water. Cold shudders ran through their bones.

Nobody spoke to Mrs Fabyash. They didn't even look in her direction so that she wouldn't suspect anything. Quietly and with hurried steps they left the cabin.

For a whole day they searched for Fabyash, calling out his name in case he might hear them, peering into every nook and corner, looking under cases and tarpaulins as if it was possible for him to be hiding there—but all was in vain. They even looked into the sea as if they expected to see him there. But the sea lay innocently and calmly holding the sun in its lap and playing hide-and-seek with it; it told them nothing. Not a sign of Fabyash was to be found anywhere. He had disappeared without leaving a trace.

Although everyone guessed what had happened and knew that their work was useless, no one spoke openly of it and they silently continued to search for him as if they expected that after all they would still find him. Nobody went near his wife in the cabin for they didn't know what to say to her. And what, after all, could be said? What news could they give her? Nobody wanted to be the bearer of sad news and each one waited for the next man to make a move and try to comfort her. They still waited—maybe a miracle would occur. Why should they run immediately and cause the woman unnecessary pain? What was the hurry? Nobody wanted to give up hope. They even announced to themselves that, after all, Fabyash might soon be found, that he would emerge from a corner and ask: 'What has happened, people... Huh?'

But Fabyash emerged from no corner and everyone missed him. This was not the first calamity that had occurred on the ship. More than one man had disappeared in broad daylight, yet no one was missed as much as Fabyash. They were so used to him. Just as at the beginning of the journey they had become accustomed to his alarms and warnings, so too later they had grown used to his silences, his self-torture and his avoidance of everything. His melancholia had been like a loud cry that demanded a response from everyone. In such a calamity as this, Fabyash would certainly have taken the part of a gloomy prophet and tormented everyone:

'Well, didn't I know that it would end like this?' he would have taunted them. 'I foresaw everything. We are all doomed. Our fate has been sealed.'

After a day of searching for Fabyash the people went down to their cabins. The only lamp in the long, narrow passageway burnt dimly as if in mourning for someone and around it hung a damp, hot odour, while the door of Fabyash's cabin was flung open as if someone had broken out by force. Mrs Fabyash was sitting alone on the edge of her bunk; with all that remained of her strength she had slid off her bunk, but her legs wouldn't carry her when she had no one to support her and she had fallen back.

They wanted to comfort her, to think up some story, but as soon as they met her eyes staring so intently and implacably with such cold, sober clarity, words failed them. Even Mrs Hudess who always told every person the blunt truth and was able to settle her own affairs—even she could not open her mouth and her tongue couldn't form words when she met Mrs Fabyash's eyes. She even had a lie ready and wore a smile on her open face, but the lie remained stuck in her throat and the smile froze on her face. Mrs Fabyash's eyes gazed with such a merciless coldness and seemed to say that no one should trouble themselves to conceal the truth. It would be a waste of time. She knew everything. She pointed dumbly to her stricken legs and begged to be taken up on deck.

But they didn't want to do it and brushing aside her demand, they still attempted to conceal the truth from her. They were not certain, still hoping, still deluding themselves that the whole thing was a mistake. Wearily they sat down near Mrs Fabyash and, looking stiffly ahead, began to talk about other matters so as to banish Fabyash from their minds. They could certainly have saved him if only they had paid some attention to him. The thought gnawed at their hearts and weighed heavily on their consciences never leaving them for a second. They talked of various things, of their homes that had been destroyed, of the fate that had befallen so many enemies of Israel, ardent followers of Hitler—may God extinguish his very name! And of the fate that awaited Hitler who would suffer like the other Hamans who had tried to exterminate and destroy the Jewish people. They talked for so long that at length they came to the land to which they were travelling.

Bronya Feldbaum said that in the new country she would open a confectionery shop. She said she would be good at that. Her black eyes glanced vivaciously and, stretching out her full, womanly throat, she said that she would always have a full shop for she knew how to attract young men and how to turn their foolish heads. Never again would she live on the land amongst peasants and ruin her remaining years. But her husband, Marcus, who generally remained silent interrupted her and would not let her finish.

'And I will settle on the land, so long as I live!' He became furious and his large, murky eyes wandered far away and became quite green and they reminded one of the Ukrainian fields whence he came.

'I will work on the land! I won't be talked out of that by anyone.'

He said no more, unable to bring out any more

words. Always calm, blunt and stolid, a man without any bitterness, his anger came very slowly and more than a few words he couldn't muster. His wife had upset him, hoping to turn him away from what he wanted to do, to twist him round her finger as she was wont to do. And so he spoke of the soil in great righteousness and excitement but he didn't know how to continue, what to say, to justify himself.

But he had no need to justify himself because everybody understood him. Rockman agreed with him and wished that he, himself, knew something about the land. Then he would go to the country without asking anyone's advice. But unfortunately nothing remained to him now but to start again in business.

As they talked amongst themselves, discussing what they would do in the new land, Mrs Fabyash suddenly sighed deeply.

'Ah, what misfortunes have befallen me!' She had realised all the miseries that she would have to face alone.

'Why did this have to happen to me, Almighty God? Why? Am I more sinful than others? It is more than a sick, broken woman can bear. It is too much for one person. Faithful Father in Heaven.'

And she began to sob. She sobbed quietly and for

a long time, and it seemed that all the tears that she had held back for so long had welled up in her and now poured out.

Everyone else became silent; speech had disappeared. No other sounds were heard but the throbbing of the ship's engines and the quiet, drawn-out, suppressed whimpering of Mrs Fabyash. The others became ashamed of themselves, of the idle talk they had indulged in. They were weighed down with guilt.

But Mrs Fabyash did not stop; she made up for all the time that she had remained silent. Everything gathered together in one painful knot that choked her and demanded a way out. All this time she had never mentioned the misfortune that had affected her legs, not saying a word as though that didn't matter. But now she pointed to her legs and cried and sobbed. Fear overpowered her; her last support had been torn away and now she was absolutely alone. It seemed as if only now had it become clear to her that she was a cripple. Although her husband hadn't glanced at her and she had not spoken to him, now that she felt how alone she was, that there was no longer anyone to even hand her anything, she saw her fate.

'What am I to do?' she wept and rocked to and fro like the pendulum of a clock.

'What am I to do? How will I get on now? Who will give me anything? I am afraid. I'm so very frightened. I am a cripple...I can't move my legs... They are as heavy as wood...They are not my legs any longer!'

The people sat in her cabin all night and only at daybreak did they go to rest. Although their eyes began to stick from fatigue and their tired limbs ached for sleep, no one was able to close his eyes. The story of Fabyash never left their minds. The thought that he had done away with himself was frightening and cast an ominous shadow before them, and they only recovered when it appeared possible that Fabyash had accidentally fallen into the water.

This was revealed when Ida, while walking on the deck, found Fabyash's wet and crumpled hat. This was after a storm had swept and rocked the ship and everyone had been certain that the end had come. The storm had begun as they stood in a queue near the dining room waiting for the cook to distribute the stew. Since the previous morning no food had been issued and just as they were ready to sit down at the tables the door was flung open with a bang and it flapped aimlessly in the wind like the broken wing of a bird. Then the door closed with a sharp crack and it became silent again—as if nothing had happened.

That was how it started and soon one of the big wooden tables rose from its place like a living thing and heaved into the air so that rusty tin plates and spoons rattled, danced and fell to the floor with a crash. Although they held on to the plates with all their might, nevertheless the food spilled over the floor. The ship reeled to one side and they all lost their balance and fell upon each other, sliding over the food, so that it seemed as though the world had turned upside down.

'It's starting again!' they groaned. 'If only it would bring rain!'

The passengers reached the door but it was closed as if some evil power was holding it with such determination that it could never be pulled open. When at last it was opened everybody was pushed back, then flung forward with such impetus that it seemed as if they were forcibly thrown out.

The wind screamed angrily as it swept the deck catching them in front and behind and throwing them off their feet. Here the wind pushed them and hurried them forward; there it impeded their progress and drove them back so that they had to battle along. It roared and cracked like many whips and soon the deck was covered in water.

The ship writhed, suspended in mid-air and then fell helplessly into the yawning abyss. From the sea poured waves of malevolent white foam that ran and jumped over each other with wild shrieks as if they were ready to devour and destroy everything in their path. Then rain fell without a pause. Heavy cool threads of water seemed to reach from sky to sea and from sea to sky as if a vast, unseen hand wanted to pattern the empty air. It appeared that the sky that was bulging with water wanted to join the sea in one deluge that would embrace everything.

Seasickness assailed the passengers. Everybody was sick and some staggered about like drunken people while others moved as if delirious and on the verge of collapse. Although they had long waited for rain, hoping that it would refresh everything and allay their thirst, now everything turned out badly. The rain that had once so pleasantly soothed the skin now brought new sorrows and the old ones were forgotten.

Nathan seached for Ida but he couldn't find her anywhere. She was, like the others, lying on her bunk in the cabin and not moving out. He was overcome by apprehension. Previously when the seas had raged he had always been together with her but now she was not with him.

It was only when the sea again became calm that he met her accidentally on the deck. She was very pale and his heart began to pound; he was so alarmed that he didn't know what to do. In his anxiety and bewilderment he involuntarily nodded his head to her in greeting as one does when a familiar face is met with unexpectedly. But quickly he realised how childishly and foolishly he had behaved and he flushed crimson to his ears. Ida made no reply, but he caught the flickering smile on her face as she passed by.

She had noticed his foolish conduct and was laughing at him.

Nathan followed Ida, watching her striding over the deck that was still wet and smelt freshly of rain. She followed the narrow passage between the lifeboats and all the time his longing for her grew stronger. He felt that he couldn't live without her.

He saw Ida bend down, pick up something and then her whole body shuddered. He came up to her quickly and saw that she held Fabyash's hat in her hand, so crumpled and soaked that it looked like a wet, faded rag.

Where the hat had come from, where the rain had brought it from nobody could guess although each had a different theory. Certainly the hat had been hanging on a lifeboat and the rain had washed it down. This relic of a living Fabyash cast fear, yet they were glad of it and it lifted them with some hope from their bitter mood. Now everyone felt certain that Fabyash hadn't done away with himself, that an accident had occurred; he had slipped. And this could happen to anybody.

No one wanted to dig too deeply or give too much thought to the matter. As soon as someone dropped a word that Fabyash had probably slipped and lost his hat everybody readily accepted the idea. Although it didn't sound reasonable and it was quite evident that this was only a cover to conceal the real facts, yet they caught hold of it with all their might. Mrs Hudess even remembered that on the night of the tragedy she heard a voice calling. Up to now she hadn't said a word to anyone because she didn't know for certain that it wasn't a dream. But now she knew that it was no dream.

'I heard someone groaning,' Mrs Hudess related. 'I heard someone distinctly calling. "Help! Save me!" I was then barely awake and I thought it was just a dream. But the voice continued to call, always more softly, until it ceased altogether. "Save me, people!" It follows me still as though I have just this moment heard it. I remained silent about it all this time because I didn't know whether it was only my imagination. I thought to myself that Fabyash had contemplated something and at the last moment changed his mind and called for help. But now I am certain that he slipped. The tragedy occurred at night when it was dark and he was alone on the deck. He took one careless step...I can imagine the suffering that he went through in his last moments. I am nearly out of my senses. If he will pardon me, Fabyash had wretched luck—may it never befall another man.'

They all stood around Mrs Hudess. And though some believed her and others didn't, it was still good to listen to her.

'Of course it must have happened like that,' someone in the circle said. 'A Jew wouldn't do a thing like that. How else could it happen? It isn't permissible for a Jew.'

Reb Zainval Rockman took away the hat that Fabyash had left and locked it in his suitcase.

CHAPTER XII

As Fabyash was no longer on the ship and there was no one else to demand an answer to the question of how the endless wanderings over the sea would end, everyone more than ever became afraid of the morrow.

More than ever they wanted to know what was happening and the idea of going to the captain to demand an answer in clear, unmistakable words grew on them.

They continually talked about it and pondered over it. Mrs Hudess, who always prided herself on hating underhand methods, began to suggest to Bronya that it would not be wrong for her, Bronya, to go to the captain and try to talk to him. Before then

Mrs Hudess had heard people talk secretly about sending Bronya to the captain; but she had not been in agreement. She couldn't accept the idea because in her eyes Bronya was an empty babbler and the whole idea just idle talk.

But now she looked at the proposition with different eyes. Mrs Hudess, who regarded herself as a forthright person, one who always spoke the unvarnished truth, couldn't bear the way the proposal was being discussed secretly, whispered in corners, as if they were ashamed of it.

'I'm an open book, a plain, straightforward person,' she said. 'As you see me, you can take me. I have always told the truth and more than once paid dearly for it. I am not one of those people who go behind others' backs. With me, what is on my chest is on my tongue! Do you want to kill the chicken without letting blood? This is a time of sorrow and we shouldn't be playing at blindman's buff.'

Now Mrs Hudess began to think highly of Bronya, even overlooking her sins, and she lauded her to the skies.

'A real doll! As pretty as a picture,' she praised her lavishly. 'She has a face as bright as the sun. You can't look into either! They say that in her Galicia the doctors would have given their lives away for her.

And she has a well-oiled mouth. With such a clever tongue one can't get lost anywhere. With her regal bearing she could live in the finest houses. She could be sent not only to a captain but to a king.'

When they heard such words, not from just anyone, but from Mrs Hudess, the people gathered more courage and began to view the proposition in a favourable light. And Rockman said, on the spot, that Mrs Hudess was right and repeated her words.

'This is a time of sorrow,' he said, as if answering himself, 'and one shouldn't play blindman's buff. And what sort of sin is it when it is all said and done for Bronya to go to the captain and talk to him? I can't see any evil in that.'

Mrs Hudess spoke to Bronya. She couldn't restrain her feelings and she poured such a stream of praise over her that Bronya blushed crimson like a little girl. Bronya was elated and unable to conceal her pleasure. She said that she would go to the captain, that it was no trouble for her—and even now, before she went, she already had the captain eating out of her hands. She could be relied upon to make him talk, have no fear of that; Bronya was the right person for the job.

Bronya gained a sense of self-importance and thought nobody could be compared with her. Those who had shown her scant respect and insulted her would soon find out who she was. She felt the great responsibility that rested on her shoulders. She alone had been chosen from all the others. She towered above everybody, feeling that they were all in her debt, that she could treat them as she wished.

She began to dress in readiness to go to the captain. With curl papers she coaxed curls and waves into her short trimmed hair. She tied a ribbon around her head and became so excited in dressing and getting ready that she took a long time and almost forgot the great responsibility that had been placed upon her. She paraded up and down the ship, dressed gaudily in all her bits and pieces, talking loudly in Polish, and when Rockman approached her she gave herself so many coquettish airs that he fell back, thoroughly embarrassed. After this performance the people began to joke with Rockman.

'It looks as if she likes you, Reb Zainval! What are you so embarrassed about? You are a handsome man and the young woman is yearning for you.'

Bronya returned from the captain with a great secret that she wouldn't divulge to anyone. She had a delighted expression, her head and shoulders quivered with joy, her piercing black eyes overflowed with pleasure. She wouldn't talk to just anyone—

she wouldn't tell just anyone of the things she had achieved with the captain. She kept the secret locked within herself, talking in riddles and hints, and it took a long time before anything could be coaxed out of her. After every few words that were extracted from her she repeated the same tale.

'Of all people, he's a captain!' She winked vivaciously. 'Anything seems to be called a captain these days. I'm sure the captain has never seen a woman before. Otherwise he wouldn't blush like a boy or a dunce in the first grade. Who could compare that man with one of our own captains? He's so phlegmatic that he doesn't know when to kiss a lady's hand. I've never met one like that before.'

Nothing else seemed to be in her mind, and to all the important questions she had no proper answer. They had to have the patience of Job to listen to all the foolishness that she uttered. She kept pouring out wonders: how she had awakened the captain from his sleep and made of him a gentleman like other men.

When she came into his cabin he hardly glanced at her, not even rising to give her a chair. But they could rely on her: Bronya knew how to handle men so that they would fall to their knees before her. Oh, those men, she knows them well! All that a woman has to do is to show some indifference, wear a cold mask on her face, and they run after her like foolish sheep. She gave that captain, that ignorant boor, a proper talking to and taught him some good manners—a little *bon ton*! And in the end he would hardly let her go and implored her to stay, with tears in his eyes, not like a captain but like a schoolboy.

On the spot he had fallen in love with her, head over heels. Now she has him firmly in the palm of her hand; he lies at her feet and she can do what she likes with him. Everything happened as she foretold. He only let her go after she promised that she would meet him again. What a piece of impudence! It wouldn't even occur to her to see him again. Although he was an unusual type, the like of whom she had never met before, he didn't interest her in the least. Naturally, she had promised to see him again, but as if she had nothing better to do than that!

With her last words she shrugged her soft, womanly shoulders sulkily and coquettishly, as though to say, 'I am not as mad as all that.' She had made the best of her opportunity to keep everyone around her, to enjoy the feeling that she was the leading lady. Everybody looked her straight in the eyes and she wanted to continue to stretch out the story. But the patience of her audience was ebbing, and someone interrupted her.

'What sort of nonsense are you talking? What sort of rubbish are you pouring into my weak head? Who can be as light-hearted as she. It would be better if you would tell us what you found out from the captain. What's the good of all this nonsense? "*Bon ton, bon ton*! Captain, captain!" Look at this addled Galician! Really it takes all kinds—a world of little worlds.'

Those words brought Bronya back down to earth. She was bewildered, her tongue was tied, sticking in her mouth, and she stammered. She no longer knew what she was talking about. The words had come so unexpectedly and they seemed so unjust to her that tears welled in her eyes. She didn't want to say any more. Tediously and with the use of many wiles they learned that the captain had told her that they were not far from a port. Another twenty-four hours, or at the most forty-eight hours, and they would reach a port.

The passengers felt almost sorry that they had chosen her for such an important mission. Somehow they couldn't believe her words. They felt no confidence in her and they knew that what she had said might have no truth at all. But they had no alternative so they looked her straight in the face and accepted everything she said as good currency. And then, if some still doubted, they were shouted down.

'A young woman comes along and talks plain words and someone already wants to twist them. Have you ever heard of such a thing?'

The joy was really deep and it increased when Reb Lazar, saying his prayers in the morning, actually saw several white seabirds. This was really the best proof that they were not far from the shore.

Reb Lazar that morning, as was his custom, awoke early, walked on the deck and looked into the Holy Book. Then he began to pray. The sun had risen like a full goblet of wine that had overflowed and flooded a large part of the sky. The sea was warming itself in the first rays of the sun, lying stretched out like a mighty silvery fish. The water was still sleepy, its drowsy ripples and swellings shimmering. When Reb Lazar saw the seabirds he reflected that they were, as in Noah's Ark, the first messengers of the land. Joy flowed through him, pervading every part of his body. He wanted to share his joy with someone as quickly as he could, but he wouldn't interrupt his prayers. Quietly and with closed eyes he recited the morning prayers without running to tell anyone. When he had finished he unwrapped his phylacteries and folded his large prayer shawl with the silvery bands that was yellow and grey with use and smelt of melting candles and passionate prayers. Only then did he hurry to relate his news.

Everybody then watched the seagulls that followed the ship, cutting the sunny air with straight and curving lines, swooping up and down and demanding food. But the ship didn't have food enough for itself, let alone any to throw to the birds as they flew tiredly after the ship, screeching hungrily in pitiful voices. Now and then a bird would drop to the sea as if it had been shot. Nearly all the morning the birds never left the ship. They came closer and closer to the people on deck, saying something to them in their bird language. Their voices rose higher as they hung in the sunny air with white, out-spread, cleanly washed wings.

The people were now certain that Bronya had invented no lie and that they were close to land. And the ship, which had been silent for so long, never uttering a cry, wailed hoarsely like a lost animal that has again found its lair. In the distance, on the sea, something black was seen. The passengers became alarmed, not knowing what it could be. And the fears grew when they noticed that their own ship, that had moved slowly all the time, now gathered speed as if it was running away from something. In great fear they stared at the dark speck that swayed gently as if anchored on the sea. It soon became clear that the speck was a ship and only when it was discovered that the ship was not an enemy one, that there was no reason for alarm, was calm restored.

For quite a time they saw the ship on the horizon and then it disappeared as suddenly as it had come. Together with the ship the birds vanished as if they had been wafted away by a magic hand. The people looked everywhere for them, running from one end of the ship to the other, peering into the distance, but they were nowhere to be seen. A great longing for the birds that had brought the first promise of land seized hold of the people on board. They longed for their hungry cries, for their strange bird language that told of the land, and their sudden disappearance left an oppressive emptiness in their hearts.

But the oppressiveness soon vanished and great happiness surged through them all so that they could not remain still for one moment. They ran after each other to announce the good news, although everyone already knew it. The appearance of the seabirds and the ship had made them forget about the land which was now surely quite close! The first delirious overpowering wave of excitement over, the realisation that they had been saved shone out. Why then is their joy so quiet? Why don't they embrace each other and dance with joy? Why do they stand with folded arms and do nothing? They should pull themselves together and get ready to land. They should pack their pitiful handfuls of rags.

Rejoicing swept the ship. They never tired of talking of the great event; they interpreted it this way and that, discussing every detail of their salvation. They repeated the same thing over and over again for the hundredth time. They threw themselves upon each other, embraced warmly, kissed passionately and tears ran from their eyes in their happiness. They thanked the Creator and nothing could silence them. In the midst of their tears they talked incessantly of the seabirds and the ship that they had seen. Rarely had they met with a ship on their long journey. All the signs surely meant that their release was not far away.

Woe to him who attempted to let drop a word doubting whether they would be admitted into a port. They had been tossed around everywhere, he said. In Greece they had only wanted to get rid of them. They had sent them away and washed their hands of the whole business. But nobody wanted to listen to him and he was silenced.

'Now, there he goes!' they shouted him down. 'A new moaner has arisen, God help us!'

CHAPTER XIII

When the first wave of joy had passed and they became accustomed to the idea that they had been saved, the people slowly returned to their cabins. Each one began to handle his own few possessions. It was a long time since they had looked at them and they lay forgotten in cases under the bunks.

Now the cases were taken out, dusted and aired to get rid of the mustiness. Their few, pitiful belongings that recently had seemed worthless had once more become of great value to them and each person trembled with excitement over every little thing. Each one made up his account, sorting out his few possessions, and they all became so absorbed in their work that they forgot everything else.

Mrs Hudess was famous as a good housewife who could do anything with her two strong hands. She swiftly and with much noise and bustle tackled her case. Everything crackled under her hands and she was the first ready. Before anyone else could turn around she had finished with everything and began to attend to her two daughters. Soon the two little girls were arrayed in clean dresses and pinafores just as if it were the eve of the Sabbath, before the lighting of the candles. Then the children went on playing with their doll. The younger one dressed the doll just as her mother had dressed her. She put on a new dress and apron and tied a ribbon in its hair. She talked to the doll in the same way as her mother had talked to her:

'My treasure. Precious.' She hugged the doll close to her. 'A blessing on your head! My heart is full when I look at you. And I only saved you by a hair's breadth. But where has your father got to, Good God in Heaven?'

Mrs Hudess had recently become devout and made her little daughters recite aloud the evening prayer before going to bed. Now, in her great joy, she hardly knew what she was doing and she did many things that were unusual for her. She looked very excited, talked without ceasing in the most extravagant way, screeched and laughed and poked her nose into everything. Without being asked she took upon herself the role of mother and looked after everybody.

And like a good but strict mother who stops at nothing, speaks out bluntly, even dressing down her grown-up sons, the fathers of children themselves— so Mrs Hudess stopped at nothing, shouted at and commanded everybody. Her pride in coming from a big city, in being a Warsaw lady, reawakened and she became a great expert on everything under the sun, although nobody wanted any of her advice. This one she reprimanded, the other she praised. Whenever she saw something that displeased her she slapped the person concerned, with a pretence of good humour, and her thin, wrinkled hands, in spite of everything, had still not lost their motherly assurance and warmth. She didn't even pause before the dignified and well-respected Rockman, but she admonished him for his grubby collar. She told him to take it off and she would wash it. This was very much out of place and Rockman was terribly embarrassed and to hide his embarrassment he gravely continued to stroke his well-cared-for, spade-shaped beard, without answering her.

Bronya made enough commotion for a whole

work-room. Flustered and dishevelled, she wandered about in a loose dressing-gown, wasting plenty of time, although everyone else hurried as if they were afraid of missing something. Around her lay scattered all her possessions: dresses, blouses, stockings, brassieres, all her bits and pieces. Nobody else had a decent bit of apparel but Bronya wanted for nothing. She could hardly attend to all the things she had to do, sorting, mending and packing. Her piece of blurred, broken mirror stood before her all the time and she was always glancing into it. She took out of her case a bit of coloured, scented soap— God only knows where she had got that from. She held it carefully in her hand and looked after it like the eyes in her head. She also dug out a jacket that she had made from some of her husband's clothes, a jacket of a thousand charms. She held it against her and posed before the broken mirror with many little feminine movements and gestures as she asked Mrs Hudess how it suited her. And Mrs Hudess had to confess that it was very charming. She became very excited and was unable to tear her eyes away from the jacket.

'This young woman can take snow and make noodles from it.' Her eyes glittered with excitement as she spoke. 'And she can put together a ribbon and a rag and from nothing make something that is charming. It's a heaven-sent gift!'

But Mrs Hudess couldn't spend much time with Bronya as she was in a great hurry to dash into Mrs Fabyash's cabin to see how she was getting on. She knew this would be a difficult job and she had been putting it off. But she hadn't forgotten Mrs Fabyash. She had come to get Bronya to go with her and she almost forcibly tore her away from her bits and pieces that had absorbed her with all her heart and soul.

As usual, Mrs Fabyash was sitting on her bunk, her heavy, crippled feet resting on the floor. When the two women came in she didn't even lift her eyes to glance at them. She had heard about everything and she didn't listen very carefully to what Mrs Hudess poured into her ears. But Mrs Hudess, not abashed, never tired of repeating the same thing over and over again. She almost talked herself to death until she had had enough of it and complained to Mrs Fabyash.

'Why don't you answer me,' she burst out in apparent vexation. 'I'm tired of talking all the time. I've already strained my heart!'

In the end she succeeded in forcing a word out of Mrs Fabyash. It was all the same to her and to everything that Mrs Hudess told her she made the same answer.

'What difference does it make to me? It's all the same to me. It's very nice of you to have come. But for me there is nothing to live for.'

Mrs Hudess summoned the courage to interrupt her.

'Now, now, don't say that! Don't sin with such words. What sort of talk is this? God knows I don't think you know yourself what you are saying.'

Mrs Hudess began to stammer, not being brazen enough to talk unrestrainedly to Mrs Fabyash. She felt that anything she could say was not enough, was superfluous. It was only self-deception for there were really no words to comfort her, but nevertheless she didn't stop. While she was speaking she gathered more courage and raised her voice higher.

'Don't pretend!' she lectured Mrs Fabyash, feigning anger, 'You want to live all right. Everybody wants to live. That's the way of the world. Don't tell stories, because nobody will believe you.'

Mrs Hudess became silent, sighed deeply and added, 'When my husband, God bless him, was torn away from me I also thought that the world was finished for me but as you see I am still living.

We forget. Life is stronger than everything else, believe me!'

It was noble of Mrs Hudess to have bared her own wounds and caused herself pain to make it easier for the other woman. Mrs Fabyash understood that and she allowed the two women to gather her few possessions. Quickly and nimbly Mrs Hudess set to work on the pitiful belongings. When she came across Fabyash's and the children's things she quickly hid them, pushing them right under everything else, so that Mrs Fabyash wouldn't have them before her eyes. Bronya helped her, doing everything that she was told. As soon as she was finished, Mrs Hudess approached Mrs Fabyash and insisted on her changing her dress and combing her hair.

'A person must take herself in hand!' Mrs Hudess said. 'One shouldn't neglect one's self! Now you're beginning to look more like yourself again. One could hardly recognise you. A pity there isn't a mirror that you could look into!'

Mrs Hudess's words, the devotion and loyalty with which she busied herself, and her anxious face touched Mrs Fabyash and she smiled faintly. Although nothing mattered to her any more, tired and sick of everything as she was since her life had lost its meaning, it gave her some pleasure that people were still interested in her and she couldn't restrain the broken smile, like a terminally sick person who feels better for a moment. But she soon felt lost again and had no more strength to listen to this feigned brave talk. She begged Mrs Hudess: 'Leave me alone. What do you want of me?'

But Mrs Hudess gave her no rest. She had seen her faint, twisted smile and with her strong hands she caught her under one arm and beckoned Bronya to take the other. The two women then took Mrs Fabyash out into the passageway.

When the eminent Warsaw doctor saw the women he ran towards them. He was now clean and neatly dressed. His silvery hair was carefully combed, his thick aristocratic moustache brushed and his black, broad-brimmed artist's hat shone. But somehow this new look didn't suit him. Although he had always talked of hygiene, warning everyone else to keep clean so as to avoid infections, he had always neglected himself. As often happens, he never saw his own faults but always those of others. Neatly groomed, as he was now, he looked uncomfortable, as though he didn't belong to himself and was in another's skin. It was apparent that his new-found neatness wouldn't last long. His well-combed hair, the brushed moustache, the good-humoured smile in the half-senile eyes all together reminded one of a child who had been forcibly washed by its mother and dressed up for an occasion; it wouldn't be long before the child got himself grubby again.

When Mrs Hudess saw the doctor she remarked to the women, and particularly to Mrs Fabyash, that some comfort could be drawn: 'There goes the doctor with his instruments. As always, misfortune goes with misfortune, the blind leads the lame. Look how his wife has decked him out! Everyone carries a load of troubles and he's well loaded. Such a learned man too! He still thinks that his son is alive.'

The doctor met the women joyfully and with outstretched arms.

'That's good,' he called to them in his careful, studied Polish. 'That's nice, you treasures! You are such dear children.'

One after the other he gave them a fatherly pinch on the cheek and addressed himself to Mrs Fabyash.

'You must walk!' he said to her, speaking more familiarly in his great joy. 'Never sit too long in one spot. If you don't help yourself nobody else will help you, not even the greatest specialists. You must exercise. You must walk although it might tire you. Otherwise you will lose all the strength in your legs!'

Seeing the doctor's great cheerfulness Mrs Fabyash became infected by it and her eyes lit up in a lively glance. But soon she remembered her great sorrows and she was ashamed of herself. She became so obstinate the women had to take her back into the cabin. Mrs Fabyash sat there hardly speaking a word to anyone. But sometimes she spoke to Ida, who rarely went up on deck, for all the excitement meant nothing to her. More than ever on the long voyage Ida now remembered her husband, Hershl, and her little daughter, Sarah. They never left her mind for one moment. Everyone, more now than ever before, thought of their own dear ones who had remained somewhere over there in the hell on the other side of the sea, yet Ida suffered more than anyone else. Sarah and Hershl stood vividly before her eyes as if she had just seen them, just that moment spoken to them. Sometimes they stood so life-like before her that she longed to talk to them. But sometimes they were so far away that she couldn't remember how they looked, and she was plunged into great fear. She thought that by losing them from her memory she had lost them forever.

Her conscience tortured her and she could find no peace. She imagined that everyone was being punished because of her. Her child's pink hair-ribbon that she always carried in her bosom scolded her, always oppressed her and never allowed her to breathe freely; it talked to her with child-like tones so that she clearly heard her child's voice.

Sometimes when Ida went on deck to talk to the women Nathan would see her. Her full lips, chapped by the sun and wind were pale and colourless, and their very pallor drew Nathan more than ever to them, filling him with a great sorrow. He felt full of pity for her. She was thin and bony. Her laughing snub-nose, her pale amber eyes that had once wrinkled with laughter and merriment or turned into thin slits of anger and malice were now dull and tearful with grief.

Ida's appearance now reminded Nathan of his wife and child, of his home, and he felt an aching longing to cast everything to the wind and go to her. The cleft in her lips that had always caused him such unrest now filled him with pain, a pain that choked in him, suffocated him, as it searched for a way out. He envied the people who could talk to her, who could stand so close to her. He alone had to stay at a distance. And not only was he jealous of those people—he envied the very walls against which Ida leaned and he envied the rails that Ida's hands clasped. Why was he less worthy than those others who could be so close to her and talk so freely with her? Why were they better than he?

In Ida, Nathan now saw the old country, his father-in-law's house where he had lived for years. More than once he wanted to go to her. He had much to tell her, a great many thoughts had accumulated in him during the time that they had not spoken. What good was it doing, this keeping away from her? But when he observed her stubbornness, her enormous stubbornness, his mind became empty, his thoughts left him and he became confused.

Ida was obstinate and she wouldn't see him. She made it clear to him in every gesture and above all in her hasty, spiteful shrug of the shoulders whenever she passed him. In that shrug lay a world of protest. But despite her malicious stubbornness Nathan could feel that she was suffering and that she yearned to meet him. Only some hidden power prevented her.

Nathan reproached himself that he always had her in his mind and could not stop thinking of her. But his anxiety about her was always with him. His large, grey eyes that were almost white, his hunched shoulders, his sunken, pale, unshaven face, his thin, wan appearance—everything spoke of his anxiety about her. She remained the only one left to him and he had to look after her. And especially now that the port was so near.

Although no one knew which port they were bound for, they had prepared themselves for the end of the journey. Nobody had noticed that the sailors were watching the passengers with astonishment, not able to make out why they had got themselves ready to go ashore. They didn't see the mocking, bitter light in the eyes of the sailors who waited to see what would be the end of it all. Who can tell what malicious people have in their minds? Nobody had time to watch the sailors, nobody even glanced at them.

At every moment another person appeared on deck in crumpled clothes that had lain for weeks in a corner where nobody had so much as looked. Although they tried to smooth out the creases in their clothes and to get rid of the damp, mouldy aroma that clung to them, no one succeeded. The old ragged clothes, stained and full of rents, suggested no special holiday but rather leaving a hospital after a long illness. Marcus Feldbaum's green hunting cap was so big on him that it covered his thin, under-nourished face the size of a fist, and fell over his ears like a hat on a child after a severe illness. It hung on his head like an upturned pot on a post. Noah's open-necked shirt ill-matched his shiny, well-worn black suit. Both the ill-fitting suit and the crumpled, grubby collar added years to his appearance. And Rockman's respectable, new, black hat that he wore only on holy days swam loosely on his head and looked so comical that his face became severe and angry. He now saw how thin he had become, just flesh and bones.

The clothes changed everyone in a remarkable fashion and called forth a new regard one for the other. Now that they had cast off the rags that they had constantly worn on the ship as if they had grown to their skins, and dressed in their best clothes a strangeness crept in amongst them and the old familiarity disappeared. It seemed as if they had never known each other before. Each was a world unto himself. Although fear had left their faces, sorrow was written there—sorrow and earnestness. It was no longer a large family with the same worries and hopes, but many little families with their own separate worries and hopes.

Meanwhile the ship trudged on for another day and another night and still no land was sighted. A tiny thought invaded everyone's mind. It sharply and stubbornly turned like a little, poisonous needle, first slowly and uncertainly, then more strongly and insistently.

Perhaps...Perhaps the whole story is a lie, a lie from beginning to end. Perhaps Bronya...who knew what the captain told her? Who can rely on Bronya! Perhaps she made up the whole story. That woman has no stability. She carries around empty stories and she doesn't know where she is.

CHAPTER XIV

The sunset was very red that night. The wind that had blown for three days didn't stop for one minute and it lashed the face sharply. It made mountains out of the waves, piled them together in heaps, built up tower upon tower of clear crystal, then dashed them down and sucked them into the depths as though into great open caves. The ship lurched drunkenly, staggered, fell in its tracks, buried itself in the lap of the ocean, as sometimes a hunted, tired animal about to surrender will bury itself in mother earth and not stir from the spot.

The sun, an enormous fiery globe, hung heavily over the sea, unwilling to leave the heavens to extinguish itself in the troubled waters. The red, glowing

sun, a round, flaming hole in the dome of the blue
heavens was mirrored in the sea, where it set fire to
the water and bathed the ship so that at any moment
it seemed that it might burst into flames. The sun
and the sky lay so close to the people on deck that it
appeared that they could stretch out their hands and
touch them with their fingers.

Then the sun went down, subsiding into the sea
like a great burning hill. It was twilight. Only the sky
was still pale and hung low over the ship, stained with
red as though reflecting the far-away burning earth.

The people on the ship watched the sky descend
low over them and small, dense clouds outlined in red
looked like torn lumps of smoke that curled, twisted
and then merged. Soon the clouds were dispersed
and there lay scattered over the sky only flaming
wisps like glowing coals and burnt-out ash.

The refugees had not yet taken off their creased
and torn best clothes, as though they were waiting for
a holiday but had made a mistake with the date and
the day had not come. They didn't feel inclined to
change. They didn't want to part with those clothes
and so lose the faint hope that still burnt somewhere
deep in their hearts.

Night fell and it became very dark so that everything merged with the blackness that surrounded

them. The sea stirred thickly and heavily like tar. People on board could not be recognised. They passed each other, brushed against each other and even collided, but still they could not recognise each other. Only when a voice was heard in the black darkness was there any sign of life and only then were they sure that they were amongst living beings and not drifting shadows.

That night Mrs Hudess watched over her daughters more carefully than ever before, not leaving them alone for one moment, keeping them near her all the time as if she had a premonition that something evil might befall them.

'How long must you keep on playing?' she pleaded with the children in a voice full of anxiety. 'It's high time to go to bed.'

She recited the evening prayer with the children, slowly and carefully separating each word, before she put them to sleep. Just as she had done when they were very tiny, she undressed them herself, kissed them and fondled them and slowly lay them down in their bunks, tenderly covering them with the old tattered blankets. She turned her cheek for them to kiss and was reluctant to tear herself away. But the girls couldn't bear her talking to them like babies and they were ashamed of her caresses, now more passionate than ever—they seemed only foolish. They kissed her hastily so that she would go away.

'Now you can go, Mummy,' they begged her, 'leave us alone.'

Before Mrs Hudess went to bed she crept into Mrs Fabyash's cabin to see how she was faring.

Reb Zainval Rockman couldn't go to sleep. He wasn't at all sleepy and he couldn't understand how anyone else could be. He kept remembering Fabyash who was always on his mind. He talked to everybody and they all listened to him attentively. Nathan gave him only one ear. He stood as if on tacks and only wanted to know if Ida was asleep. Tonight more strongly than ever before he longed to find her and be close to her. He must no longer stay away from her. The resolution flared up in him, assumed definite shape, took on flesh and blood; but it soon petered out again. It seemed strange and wild and impossible to realise. Nevertheless, he felt that when he met her next he would certainly be strong enough to talk to her.

Ida too, this night, wandered alone around the ship for a long time, hoping that she would accidentally meet Nathan. In the darkness she searched for him, fearfully looking into strange faces. She was possessed by a great longing for him, by a sorrow and a fear for him that pressed heavily upon her so that she felt a sharp pain and could barely catch her breath. Nobody but Nathan remained to her. The pain cut her deeply, gave her no rest, ate into her until she could bear it no longer and exclaimed softly, 'Nathan.'

The name having escaped her lips she was startled and wanted to draw it back, but nobody had heard her voice and nobody answered her. Only the foaming sea answered, with a roar of mocking laughter as it bared its white teeth. It rose from its place, arched its mighty, black spine and wildly reached out with strong wet paws to touch the ship as if it wanted to test how much longer the ship could hold out.

All the time Ida imagined that Nathan was passing her by and she ran after him. But she was wrong. He had always been near her; she had felt his nearness, even when she had not looked in his direction. But now when she really wants him, when her anxiety for him is so deep, he is not here and he can't hear her calling him.

On this night, just as at the beginning of the journey, the people were gathered together in their cabins. And just as during the early days of the journey they talked until late into the night about the countries they had been forced to wander through since that day when they had fled their homes before the Nazi hordes. They felt towards each other a deep intimacy, a kinsmanship that could never be disturbed, a love that streamed from the depths of their hearts. They were again one big family with the same sorrows and aspirations.

As always, the chief spokesman was Reb Zainval Rockman. He invited into his cabin the Warsaw doctor, Feldbaum and Noah and he told them that Fabyash had vividly appeared before him. Yes, Fabyash! Although they were all certain that he only wanted an audience to bore with his tales, nevertheless they listened to him very carefully. And the doctor, who liked to talk a lot himself, stared into Rockman's eyes with an all-knowing, sympathetic, half-senile smile as if to say: 'I understand everything. I understand.'

The half-clever, half-senile smile caused a cold shudder to pass through Rockman and he felt bewildered. A sensible man who never lost his wits, Rockman now felt that things were happening around him that were beyond his comprehension, outside the reach of his mind. Back home in his own township he had been very highly regarded; everybody, even children, respected him. He was a peacemaker and his quiet, commonsense advice helped to straighten out the most difficult tangles with no ill will to anybody. They never had to tell him much; he guessed what was in the other's mind, exactly what he was going to say, before he opened his mouth. With his own children he had quarrelled for a long time, until at last he saw that they were not so wrong, perhaps they were even right. And then sometimes he looked into the books to discover their truths.

Although Reb Zainval Rockman tried to persuade himself that with God's help everything would be all right, he now felt that the end was near. No good could come from such endless drifting over the sea, where the waters were not safe and where every moment life was in danger. Something terrible would happen. He could read it in the faces of all the Jews who still tried to persuade themselves, just as he did, that everything was not yet lost. He looked around and by the dim light he saw their pale, bloodless faces and it struck him that they were not the faces of living beings. They were not living people who surrounded him. Even the voice of Reb Lazar, the grocer, reading from the Holy Book, rang strangely as if it came from another world. Reb Lazar, who was a humble man and always spoke softly, had a confident voice when he was reading and this voice now cast fear into everybody; but at the same time it gave them strength so that everyone became quiet and listened to him.

Nobody felt like going to bed, although they yearned to lie down on their bunks and sleep and sleep and forget everything.

It was late at night when they finally prepared to go to bed. Rockman went into his cabin, hardly able to get past the sleeping bodies on the floor. He undressed and, as his habit was, laid his clothes neatly and correctly by his side. The cabin was so crowded that every now and then someone touched another's hand or foot. Snoring and wheezing was heard and a heavy, salty odour hung in the air. A child woke from sleep and cried loudly. Someone shouted in his sleep, muttered about something for a moment as if making a confession and then lapsed into a moaning cry.

Then suddenly a loud crash drowned out everything else. The roar was as mighty and as terrifying as if the world was going under.

But the world didn't go under. Only an old Greek freighter, with its passengers and crew.

The explosions continued, following more quickly and more heavily upon each other. The sea shot into the air along with pieces of wood, iron and steel that flew far apart, scattering in all directions. Fire pierced the blackness and dismally lit up the surrounding night. Then the funnel wailed into the blackness, rising in a crescendo as if shrieking for help. But its choking, spluttering voice was soon completely cut off as if someone had forcibly stopped its mouth.

From all sides the water rushed on to the ship that was helplessly sinking without a sigh. The fire wrestled with the water, leaping from one spot to another, hiding and then reappearing. Raging flamboyantly, it thrust into the face of the night several laughing, red tongues that danced wildly, curled and twisted and then shot out again. The dense smoke was choking and suffocating; it grew and enveloped everything like a great, smoky mountain.

The water poured in—poured like an avalanche, running swiftly and strongly as if in a race, over planks, walls, sheets of iron that fell to pieces like plaster, over everything that still floated on the surface of the sea. The water pounded vehemently with the clang of iron, destroying everything in its way and in such haste that it seemed to want to make an end of everything. Mountainous walls of water, like walls of iron and steel, rose higher and higher, one above the other, tearing the weary ship limb from limb. So great was the noise and havoc that the muffled human cries could not be heard. The sounds that came from somewhere deep in the bowels of the ship were like voices from covered graves.

The sea shouted with triumph, hurried and bellowed, slobbering with joy as though satiated after a wild, drunken orgy. It seemed that the sea had broken over its shore.